Sovereign

Part Three of
The Honeycomb Trilogy

Mac Rogers

A SAMUEL FRENCH ACTING EDITION

SAMUEL
FRENCH

FOUNDED 1830

SAMUELFRENCH.COM
SAMUELFRENCH-LONDON.CO.UK

FOR PRODUCTION ENQUIRIES

UNITED STATES AND CANADA
Info@SamuelFrench.com
1-866-598-8449

UNITED KINGDOM AND EUROPE
Plays@SamuelFrench-London.co.uk
020-7255-4302

Each title is subject to availability from Samuel French, depending upon country of performance. Please be aware that *SOVEREIGN* may not be licensed by Samuel French in your territory. Professional and amateur producers should contact the nearest Samuel French office or licensing partner to verify availability.

MUSIC USE NOTE

Licensees are solely responsible for obtaining formal written permission from copyright owners to use copyrighted music in the performance of this play and are strongly cautioned to do so. If no such permission is obtained by the licensee, then the licensee must use only original music that the licensee owns and controls. Licensees are solely responsible and liable for all music clearances and shall indemnify the copyright owners of the play(s) and their licensing agent, Samuel French, against any costs, expenses, losses and liabilities arising from the use of music by licensees. Please contact the appropriate music licensing authority in your territory for the rights to any incidental music.

IMPORTANT BILLING AND CREDIT REQUIREMENTS

If you have obtained performance rights to this title, please refer to your licensing agreement for important billing and credit requirements.

THE HONEYCOMB TRILOGY was originally presented by Gideon Productions in three separate productions over the first half of 2012 at The Secret Theatre in Long Island City, New York. **ADVANCE MAN** ran in January 2012, **BLAST RADIUS** in March and April 2012, and **SOVEREIGN** in June 2012. The performances were directed by Jordana Williams, produced by Sean Willams and Shaun Bennet Fauntleroy, with sets by Sandy Yaklin, costumes by Amanda Jenks, lights by Jennifer Wilcox, sound by Jeanne Travis, props and effects by Stephanie Cox-Williams, fight choreography by Joseph Mathers, alien leg design by Zoe Morsotte, and publicity by Emily Owens PR. The Production Stage Manager was Nikki Castle. The cast was as follows:

RONNIE	Hanna Cheek
ABBIE	Stephen Heskett
FEE	Sara Thigpen
ZANDER	Matt Golden
TANYA	Medina Senghore
CLARET	Erin Jerozal
SHARP	Daryl Lathon
WILKIE	Neimah Djourabchi
BUDEEN	C. L. Weatherstone

THE HONEYCOMB TRILOGY was subsequently presented by Gideon Productions in repertory at the Gym At Judson in New York City in October and November of 2015. The performances were directed by Jordana Williams and produced by Sean Williams, Rebecca Comtois, and Mikell Kober, with sets by Sandy Yaklin, costumes by Amanda Jenks, lights by Jennifer Wilcox, sound by Jeanne Travis, blood effects by Stephanie Cox-Williams, alien leg design by Zoe Morsotte and Lauren Genutis, fight choreography by Adam Swiderski, and publicity by Emily Owens PR. The Production Stage Manager was Nikki Castle and the Assistant Director was Audrey Marshall.

RONNIE	Hanna Cheek
ABBIE	Stephen Heskett
FEE	Yeauxlanda Kay
ZANDER	Matt Golden
TANYA	Lori E. Parquet
CLARET	Erin Jerozal
SHARP	Daryl Lathon
WILKIE	Neimah Djourabchi
BUDEEN	C. L. Weatherstone

CHARACTERS

The Cooke siblings can be any race/ethnicity. It would probably work best if they look biologically related.

RONNIE COOKE – 38, female

ABBIE COOKE – 35, male

FEE – 8 years older than in *Blast Radius,* female, same ethnicity as in *Blast Radius*

ZANDER – 40s, male, any ethnicity

TANYA – 20s, female, any ethnicity

CLARET – 20s to 40s, female, any ethnicity

SHARP – 30s to 40s, male, any ethnicity

WILKIE – 30s to 40s, male, any ethnicity

BUDEEN – late 20s to 40s, male, any ethnicity

SETTING

The Cooke family's living room eight years after the events of *Blast Radius.*

ACT ONE

(Eight years have passed since the events of Blast Radius.*)*

(The former living room of the former Cooke household. Somewhat improved since Blast Radius. *Cleaner, dry. The walls decorated with pre-Honeycomb-invasion objects. One wall is dominated by a large, wooden, rough-hewn memorial: "THE 51." Among the 51 names are Jimmy, Dev, Clem... and Conor and Peck. The first right above the second.)*

(It's now arranged like a courtroom. Benches for prosecution and defense. A chair in the middle for the accused. A rough-hewn wooden throne, in which sits **RONNIE COOKE**. *A rack of reapers and bug-hunter robes along one wall.)*

*(***BUDEEN**, *dirty in the manner of a man who works outside every day and doesn't have running water, sits in the accused chair.* **FEE** *takes notes in one corner.* **TANYA** *sits on the defense bench.* **ZANDER** *stands, mid-examination.)*

ZANDER. Why don't we just start with an easy question? Does that sound good?

BUDEEN. Like what?

ZANDER. Well, like, what is your name?

BUDEEN. Budeen House Twenty.

> *(reactions around the room)*

ZANDER. All right, Budeen, you do understand that that is not your name, right?

BUDEEN. What?

ZANDER. You have a name. As a free human. Some people came to your house, about a year ago, from the Settlement Authority, right?

BUDEEN. Came to my house?

ZANDER. From the Settlement Authority, and they assigned you a new second name.

TANYA. We don't have to do this, I have the record here, Settlement Authority assigned Budeen –

ZANDER. *(overlapping)* I'm asking my questions. I'm asking my questions.

BUDEEN. It was Shannah that answered the door.

ZANDER. All right now *Shannah*, before we go on, who is Shannah?

BUDEEN. Lived with me. Mother my children.

ZANDER. Your wife.

BUDEEN. Shannah would answer the door. If people came.

ZANDER. And as your wife, Shannah would share a second name with you. Right? You follow me? What's that second name?

TANYA. I have it right here –

ZANDER. I'm asking Budeen, I'm asking the subject under questioning –

RONNIE. All right, people, you know what? I know Budeen has a second name because millions of people died so he could have it. Will someone just say what it is?

ZANDER. Sorry Ronnie.

TANYA. Simmons, Governor.

ZANDER. *(correcting himself) Governor.* Yes. Sorry.

RONNIE. Simmons. Like pulling motherfucking teeth.

BUDEEN. Sorry. It's just Shannah would answer the door.

ZANDER. So, Mr. *Simmons.* So Shannah Simmons would be your wife.

BUDEEN. What?

ZANDER. You are Budeen Simmons. Right? That's your name. So when I say "Mr. Simmons," that means I'm talking to you.

BUDEEN. All right.

ZANDER. And for the same reason, when I say "Mrs. Simmons," Budeen, I mean your wife.

BUDEEN. Shannah.

ZANDER. Yes, Shannah Simmons.

BUDEEN. Mother my children.

ZANDER. Your *wife*.

BUDEEN. All right.

ZANDER. So where is Mrs. Simmons now? Mr. Simmons? Where is your wife?

BUDEEN. Wife…

ZANDER. *(to* **RONNIE***)* Governor, we should push this to tomorrow.

RONNIE. Tomorrow's list is as long as today's. We finish.

ZANDER. Mr. Simmons: where is Shannah? Right now, at this moment: where is she? Do you understand what I'm asking you?

BUDEEN. All around my house. In my stuff.

TANYA. May I note again for the Governor's consideration that Mr. Simmons is, for a start, unable to read –

RONNIE. You get a turn. This isn't it.

ZANDER. All around your house and in your stuff. What do you mean by that, Mr. Simmons?

BUDEEN. New digger, new reaper, new turner, uh…and for the gators too…and over the windows.

ZANDER. New digger, new reaper, new turner – now these are gardening tools, correct?

BUDEEN. For the veggies, yeah.

ZANDER. So what do gardening tools have to do with your wife, Mr. Simmons?

BUDEEN. *(tapping bones on his body to indicate)* Digger, from Shannah. Reaper, from Shannah. Turner, from Shannah.

ZANDER. Her bones, you made these tools from her bones.

BUDEEN. Bones, yeah. Shannah talked for me, mostly.

ZANDER. Now you said "gators" a minute ago, what did you mean by "gators"?

BUDEEN. Gotta feed 'em 'til they're big enough.

ZANDER. Gotta feed 'em 'til they're big enough. So you fed them Mrs. Simmons' flesh. Is that right? You fed them Shannah's flesh.

*(**BUDEEN** looks at **TANYA**.)*

TANYA. *(pinching her arm)* Flesh.

BUDEEN. Oh, yeah. To the gators.

ZANDER. And "over the windows," you said Mrs. Simmons is "over the windows"?

BUDEEN. Yeah.

ZANDER. Can you explain what you mean by that?

BUDEEN. Bits down here – *(He pats his lower stomach.)* – Clean 'em, scrape 'em off, and hang 'em up in the sun 'til they're stiff like that. Then I put 'em in the windows so those Twitches can't get in.

ZANDER. So, her intestines. You put them over your windows.

*(**BUDEEN** looks at **TANYA**. She nods.)*

BUDEEN. Yeah.

ZANDER. So Mr. Simmons, if you're using your wife's bones as tools and her flesh as feed for your gators and her intestines as fencing for your windows, then I think we can say your wife is *dead*, yes? Is Shannah dead, Budeen? *(pause)*

BUDEEN. Yeah.

ZANDER. When did she die? How many days has it been?

BUDEEN. Don't know. A few.

ZANDER. And how did she die, Mr. Simmons? How did Shannah die?

BUDEEN. Cough.

ZANDER. She had the cough.

BUDEEN. So bad she had no sleep with it. I put the hot weeds on her chest like they said but Shannah used to do that for us and I'm no good at it. Then the cough was blood, then she goes on.

ZANDER. She goes on – she *died.*

BUDEEN. Yeah.

ZANDER. All right, so: when she died, Mr. Simmons, when Shannah died, did you tell anyone?

BUDEEN. Tell?

ZANDER. You know that "tell" means, right?

BUDEEN. Kids seen her go on.

ZANDER. But did you tell anyone else?

BUDEEN. Like who?

ZANDER. Like anyone in the Settlement Authority, any of the peace officers you see walking around – anyone in authority *at all.*

BUDEEN. Authority?

ZANDER. *Yes.*

BUDEEN. Bugs're gone.

(A bad moment.)

ZANDER. All right, Governor, we'll just, –

RONNIE. *(to* BUDEEN*)* What did you just say?

ZANDER. Governor, I'm almost done –

RONNIE. *(to* BUDEEN*.)* Say it again. Say what you just said.

BUDEEN. Bugs're gone. Don't have to send the body to the 'Comb anymore. Bugs're gone.

TANYA. Even if Mr. Simmons was present when the Settlement Authority announced the new regulations –

RONNIE. That's what you think when you hear "authority"? You think bugs?

BUDEEN. I don't…get it.

ZANDER. Governor, if I may.

　　　*(**RONNIE** waves for him to continue.)*

Mr. Simmons, the Code of Law governing Coral Settlement requires that when someone dies, their house must notify – *tell* – someone from the Settlement Authority so that a funeral service and a burial can be arranged. So this is very important: did you tell anyone – *anyone* – outside your house that Shannah died?

BUDEEN. I…

ZANDER. Yes or no, Mr. Simmons? It can only be yes or no.

BUDEEN. No.

ZANDER. Thank you, Mr. Simmons. Ms. Miller?

　　　*(**TANYA** looks at **BUDEEN** for a moment, considering.)*

RONNIE. We gonna do this?

TANYA. Yes, Governor.

RONNIE. Couldn't wait to interrupt when it wasn't your turn and now you don't say shit?

TANYA. Budeen, thank you for being with us today. Now I'm going to –

RONNIE. *(to **BUDEEN**)* You know a human body has dignity, don't you?

BUDEEN. What?

RONNIE. That it's something more than fucking gator feed?

FEE. *(to **RONNIE**)* Okay now.

BUDEEN. *(rising from the stool)* Look, I gotta go home. I got the kids, it's almost sunfall.

RONNIE. What makes you think you're going home?

BUDEEN. Only came 'cause the guys with reapers made me. I got the kids. There's still work.

RONNIE. *(to **TANYA**)* You really better get in there.

TANYA. Budeen, I have to ask you some questions now. All right? So why don't you answer my questions, and maybe you can go home?

BUDEEN. Nah, I gotta go now, already lost the light, I gotta *work*.

RONNIE. Well you *can't* go home, got it? So answer the questions and *sit the fuck down!*

FEE. Ronnie.

RONNIE. You know I couldn't bury my own mother, right? Did you know that?

FEE. *Ronnie.*

RONNIE. *(to* FEE*)* Why aren't you writing? Write it down.

FEE. Seriously?

RONNIE. I couldn't bury my own mother – write it down! Watched them cart her off for compost.

FEE. Yeah, all right.

> *(A bad silence as* FEE *scribbles.* TANYA *looks at* RONNIE *for permission to continue.* RONNIE *gives it.)*

TANYA. So Budeen, you said that Shannah died a few days ago?

BUDEEN. Yeah.

TANYA. So how are you? Are you all right?

BUDEEN. What?

TANYA. How do you feel?

BUDEEN. Feel?

ZANDER. Ms. Miller, don't you think it's getting a little late to waste time determining how Mr. Simmons *feels*?

BUDEEN. She worked hard. Good with the kids.

TANYA. But how do you feel? When you think about Shannah.

BUDEEN. She answered the door. Talked to people. I don't know what to say so she talked to people.

TANYA. I'm saying when you think of Shannah, Budeen, when you look around your house and you see she's not there: How do you feel? *(beat)*

BUDEEN. Cold.

TANYA. You feel cold.

BUDEEN. Cold, I don't… I don't know what to do. The kids cry, I don't know what to do.

TANYA. Have you cried?

ZANDER. Look, I'm sorry, what possible relevance –

TANYA. Have you cried, Budeen?

BUDEEN. Can't. Too old.

TANYA. That's not true. You can be sad no matter how old you are.

BUDEEN. Cold, mostly. Come inside at sunfall and she's there, and we sit together or fuck or smoke choopie or chase the kids, and that's warm. Now it's cold.

TANYA. You miss her.

BUDEEN. What?

TANYA. You wish she was still alive.

BUDEEN. Yeah, all right. I wish that.

TANYA. She meant a lot to you.

BUDEEN. Wishing's nothing. Doesn't do anything. But I wish that.

TANYA. You loved her. *(beat)* Budeen, I need you to answer out loud.

BUDEEN. Yeah.

TANYA. So then why did you cut up her body for tools and gator feed and window fencing? If you loved her, why did you do that?

BUDEEN. I don't get it.

TANYA. Doesn't it seem like, if you loved her like you say, that you'd want to bury her whole body, lovely as she was, down south in the Land of the Dead?

BUDEEN. That's crazy.

RONNIE. Excuse me?

BUDEEN. Just put her whole body in the ground? That's crazy.

TANYA. Why is that crazy? Wouldn't that show how you cared for her? There'd be a little marker there, and you could go every day to visit her if you wanted, and you'd always know she was there.

BUDEEN. I know she's there now.

TANYA. What do you mean? You cut her body to pieces. How can you know she's there?

BUDEEN. 'Cause I work with my new tools all day long, so she's there. Like she's there working with me. I see my gators fed and almost big enough for killin,' so she's there. I look at my windows and now those Twitches can't get in and scare my kids, so she's there. Like she's watching us when we sleep. Not like it was, but she's there. Shannah's there.

TANYA. All right, Budeen.

BUDEEN. She worked real hard then, she works real hard now. Don't say anything bad about her.

TANYA. We won't, Budeen.

ZANDER. Ms. Miller, should we expect to hear any evidence at all that Budeen Simmons didn't break with Settlement law this evening?

TANYA. Mr. Smith – Governor Cooke – every law has a letter and a spirit, yes? Our ancestors from the Time Before, they believed every law had it's own definition, and then behind that definition, the larger reason it existed, its *spirit.*

(Something in RONNIE*'s expression is catching her off.)*

Governor Cooke?

RONNIE. No, this is good. I'm enjoying it. Why don't you tell me what my own laws mean?

ZANDER. Well – obviously – Settlement Law was established by a whole body of –

RONNIE. No, go on. Tell me what my laws mean.

(Over the following, **SHARP** *enters quietly through the front door. He doesn't interrupt, but signals* **RONNIE.***)*

TANYA. Under the Honeycomb, when our people died, the bugs just came and took them away. No pause for grief or ceremony, just took them away for digestion in the Honeycomb. So the law Mr. Smith is talking about – you must notify authority, you must arrange funeral and burial – Settlement Authority made that law to give each person's death an individual meaning and dignity, to reclaim what the Honeycomb took from us.

ZANDER. Ms. Miller, it is now fully sundown –

TANYA. Mr. Simmons has clearly, in his own way, honored the life of Shannah Simmons. He has reincorporated the elements of her body into his life in the ways which are most meaningful to him: tools to do his work, food for the livestock that gives him his living, guards on the windows behind which his children sleep. Nothing means more to him.

ZANDER. People don't get to invent their own ways of following the law –

TANYA. I ask the Governor, I implore the Governor, to show clemency, to show mercy, and not take a man from his children who has worked hard, in his own way, to honor the spirit of her wise and extraordinary law.

*(***RONNIE*** rises and walks forward. This is the first time we see the limp.)*

RONNIE. *(to* **SHARP***)* What is it?

SHARP. It can wait.

ZANDER. Governor, we should probably conclude these proceedings –

RONNIE. Sharp: What is it?

SHARP. Skins.

RONNIE. So? Process them and get 'em in the pen.

SHARP. Not Twitches.

RONNIE. Mobile? Verbal?

SHARP. Both. We can bring 'em in when you're done.

RONNIE. Run them through processing. I can see them at the pen. *(beat)* What?

SHARP. You're gonna wanna see these yourself. *(beat)*

RONNIE. *(to ZANDER, indicating BUDEEN)* Lockup, thirty nights, thirty lashings. Get someone out to the kids, they'll stay at Schoolhouse for the duration.

TANYA. Governor, I implore you, the hardship the Simmons family will face –

RONNIE. Did you hear me say thirty and thirty? Plus Schoolhouse for the kids? For what he did? That's *nothing*! *(to BUDEEN.)* What did we rise up for, why did we burn so many bodies, why did we lose *half our number* if you're still gonna live like an animal? When someone dies, the town comes out. We wrap her up, we take her to the Land of the Dead, everyone who remembers her says something, and we put her in the ground together. 'Cause we're not *fucking parts*! *(to SHARP.)* Get him out to the PO's, tell them straight to lockup.

SHARP. And the Skins?

RONNIE. Take them around back. Don't bring them in 'til I send for you.

SHARP. Yeah.

RONNIE. And I can't see shit. Tell one of the guys to turn on the generator.

SHARP. Got it.

      (SHARP exits with BUDEEN.)

RONNIE. *(to TANYA)* You're done, right? For the day? There's not gonna be anything else from you?

TANYA. Unless you've reconsidered my petition regarding the Transitioned prisoners, then I –

RONNIE. We've been here since dawn. I haven't stretched this leg since dawn. You do not want to fuck with me.

TANYA. In that case, Governor, you didn't need to ask the question.

RONNIE. Every time there's one that should take us two minutes, they always have you.

TANYA. Yes, Governor.

ZANDER. You can't take everyone, Tanya, you have to start picking.

FEE. You'll just work until you die.

TANYA. Governor Cooke says we can find the wisdom of the world in the books from the Time Before. The ones I've read say everyone in the Time Before had someone speaking for them. No one had to stand up and answer alone.

> *(A groaning mechanical sound from outside as a number of electric lights come on.)*

RONNIE. You're done. Go home.

> *(Over the following,* **TANYA** *gathers some materials and leaves.)*

All right, Zander, what's left?

FEE. First, you sit down.

RONNIE. Forget it.

FEE. Sit down. Take weight off it.

RONNIE. I'd only have to get back up, right? Leave it.

FEE. Bullshit. The girl got in your face, you're sulking, and you don't want to sit down in front of Mr. Smith.

ZANDER. You're aware, Ronnie, that the fittest men in Coral Settlement would fight to the death for the privilege of carrying you around all day long.

> *(***RONNIE*** *steps away from the wall and straightens up with no support.)*

RONNIE. Governor.

ZANDER. Governor.

RONNIE. What's left?

ZANDER. Just bits.

RONNIE. It's not "bits," if it was "bits" you wouldn't have to say so.

ZANDER. All right, it's not bits.

RONNIE. Then you better talk fast.

ZANDER. Your Bug Hunter Corps has gone on a number of missions lately.

RONNIE. So?

ZANDER. They leave at night, they return at night.

RONNIE. My Bug Hunters aren't Council business.

ZANDER. Well, that's another issue, but I'll table that for now.

RONNIE. Aren't you sweet?

ZANDER. Are your Bug Hunters collecting and stockpiling bugwater?

RONNIE. All right.

ZANDER. Because I think I have an unimpeachable record when it comes to letting you keep your secrets, Governor. The problem arises when one of your secrets literally gives off a smell. Then the rest of us have to walk around looking at each other wondering who will be the first to mention it.

RONNIE. Anyone who asked at any time, I would've said "Yes."

ZANDER. Governor – who is likely to ask?

RONNIE. Answered your own question.

ZANDER. So that's Settlement Manager, then? "Takes life into hands each day, asking the Governor annoying questions."

RONNIE. Less annoying question is, "Why wouldn't we?" You think no one else is?

ZANDER. Who?

RONNIE. Cubano Settlement, Savannah Settlement, Wheeling Settlement, all up the coast, every farm that's still inhabited, you think they're letting their leftover bugwater just sit there?

ZANDER. But with respect, Governor: Cubano, Savannah, Wheeling…those aren't bug-nests, are they? We've visited all of them. They're sovereign states, *run by human beings.*

RONNIE. If they're doing it, we're doing it.

ZANDER. We don't know that they're doing it.

RONNIE. Why would they not be? They'd have to be fools!

ZANDER. And all those vows made standing over the charred remains of heroes "We finish this, and then never again."

RONNIE. *(massaging her leg)* What makes you think it's finished?

FEE. Sit. Sit. Now.

> *(She drags a chair over to* **RONNIE.** *They look hard at each other.* **RONNIE** *sits – but willfully in a different chair than the one* **FEE** *brought.)*

RONNIE. *(to* ZANDER.*)* You asked, I said yes. Happy?

ZANDER. People smell the bugwater, and they sit up in their houses at night after the Peace Officers go to bed asking each other the same thing: Will it happen again? Will the call go out again? Is Governor Cooke going to come sit in my front room and ask me to be a hero?

RONNIE. *(indicating the 51 memorial)* Look at the wall, Zander.

ZANDER. Yes, Governor.

RONNIE. Touch a name.

ZANDER. All right, I don't think this is necessary –

RONNIE. Pick a name, and touch it.

> *(***ZANDER** *goes to the wall and touches a name.)*

How many heroes, Zander, try to guess: how many heroes did I personally – not my lieutenants, *me* – persuade to join the Fifty-First?

ZANDER. I can't even imagine.

RONNIE. Usually with a mate, brother, sister, parent, child right next to them, trying to talk them out if it?

ZANDER. Governor, there is no one who does not deeply honor your service –

RONNIE. So wouldn't you think I would try anything I could possibly think of before ever having to do that again?

ZANDER. I do believe that.

RONNIE. Then what are we talking about?

ZANDER. Only…who will be the one to decide when we've tried everything?

RONNIE. What do I have to do to earn the trust of the people I work right next to every fucking day? Do I have to liberate the Earth a second time?

*(Over the following pause, **WILKIE** enters through the kitchen. He is dressed similarly to **SHARP**.)*

Tell me, please, that we're finally done.

ZANDER. Only one more matter.

RONNIE. What have we been doing all day? Where's "one more matter" been all day long?

ZANDER. I thought this one was best initially broached between you and me in private.

RONNIE. You mean the Council's scared to ask so you offered to soften me up. *(to **WILKIE**.)* Tell me.

WILKIE. Hi Governor.

RONNIE. Tell me.

WILKIE. Me n' Sharp have the Skins out back.

RONNIE. We're almost done here.

WILKIE. Got it, got it, got it.

ZANDER. Of course, Governor, there is a process for registering prisoners in place –

RONNIE. For fuck's sake, Zander, what's everyone scared to ask me now?

ZANDER. We need to pull more people off Miami Dig and put them back on the farms.

RONNIE. No.

ZANDER. Well respectfully I don't think you can just say "no," if I correctly understand the governing structure of Coral –

RONNIE. "If I correctly understand the governing structure" – how do you even know how to talk like that?

ZANDER. Yes, Governor, I do take your point.

RONNIE. No, actually say it: How do you know how to talk like that?

ZANDER. From reading books recovered by Miami Dig.

RONNIE. Nothing's more important that Miami Dig. Miami Dig's number one.

ZANDER. Well, I would venture to say that food is more important.

RONNIE. I'm sorry, is someone starving?

ZANDER. Infrastructure is more important.

RONNIE. *(to* **FEE***)* Ever think you'd hear "infrastructure" again?

FEE. Never heard it before.

ZANDER. The family farms, the common farms, they're producing enough now, but –

RONNIE. Who's starving?

ZANDER. They're producing enough *now*, but you have to watch how many babies are being born. You have to keep count, and you have to keep in mind that they will *grow up and have more babies.* We need bigger farms, we need to consolidate the farms that are out there under Settlement control, we need to enforce best practices for maximum crop yield –

FEE. *(to* **RONNIE***)* When does he breathe?

ZANDER. And then we'll need longboats and wider canals to move the crop and *still* have enough left over to staff a prison full of Twitches that don't know how to feed themselves! And all that takes bodies, and the only place to *get* bodies is from the hundreds we currently have digging up Miami.

RONNIE. You've given a lot of thought to how you're going to remake my Settlement, haven't you?

ZANDER. The others were frightened. I said to them, "Aren't you more frightened of just letting this situation fester?"

RONNIE. I'm curious: where and when did this conversation take place? *(pause)*

ZANDER. We have likely accomplished as much as we're going to this day.

RONNIE. Sounds good to me.

WILKIE. Shit, I'm glad that's over!

ZANDER. Welcome back, Wilkie, I'm glad your team has returned safely.

WILKIE. Hey, better than safely, man.

ZANDER. Yes.

WILKIE. We brought treats!

ZANDER. *(setting his notes on a bench)* Yes. And I'm sure at some point this evening the Governor will have you send your treats to lockup for proper documentation.

WILKIE. And I'm sure I'll do whatever the fuck Ronnie says.

ZANDER. I'll be back in the morning.

>   *(He exits out the front door as* **WILKIE** *pulls his bug-hunter cloak off and hangs it up.)*

WILKIE. Man it feels good to get that thing off.

RONNIE. Let's see 'em.

WILKIE. Now? You want 'em now? Or do you need a couple minutes? Why don't you take a couple minutes? Maybe go upstairs? Stretch out? You just got done with Shitmouth there, you probably need a couple minutes.

RONNIE. No.

WILKIE. No? Bring 'em on in?

RONNIE. Yeah, now.

WILKIE. I hope you weren't worried about me.

RONNIE. What?

WILKIE. *(meaning* **FEE***)* It's good with her, right, she knows?

>   *(***FEE** *looks up, amused.)*

RONNIE. I'll see the Skins now, please.

WILKIE. 'Cause you shouldn't've been. Worried about me. Not a scratch, not a slash, all intact!

RONNIE. Good. Good. I'm glad.

WILKIE. Yeah?

RONNIE. I'm glad you're not hurt, Wilkie.

WILKIE. You can check for yourself a little later, right?

RONNIE. Wilkie. The Skins.

WILKIE. You definitely don't need a couple minutes? If it's about the stairs I can carry you –

FEE. She doesn't need a couple minutes, Wilkie, bring them in.

WILKIE. You got it, you got it, you got it.

> *(Before **RONNIE** can react, **WILKIE** leans down to where she's sitting and kisses her.)*

Now that's what I've been missing!

> *(He exits through the kitchen door.)*

FEE. You ever just tried no man?

RONNIE. He's all right.

FEE. No man's been fine with me for a while.

RONNIE. Can't stand it. My brain races all night.

FEE. Peace of mind...

RONNIE. I don't do that in any case, so...

FEE. You wanna be standing or sitting? When they come in?

RONNIE. Sitting. Don't let them think they're a big deal.

FEE. All right. *(beat)*

RONNIE. How's um...

FEE. Little Shirley?

RONNIE. Yeah.

FEE. Good this week. Worked real hard.

RONNIE. The others?

FEE. "The others."

RONNIE. Come on, give me a break.

FEE. I mean, Ronnie, they're old enough to fetch n' carry.

RONNIE. Yeah.

FEE. Most days I don't see them when the sun's up.

RONNIE. Fuck.

FEE. It's the kind of thing you notice, not having giant flying bugs to carry the crop around anymore. You can feel it in your back. *(She looks at* **RONNIE.***)* You gonna lash me?

RONNIE. Anybody else.

FEE. I know.

RONNIE. I'll come see her. Little Shirley. Day after tomorrow. Are you back here tomorrow?

FEE. Rather not, but if you need me…

RONNIE. No, skip it, Cassie can take notes. And my big men are back, if someone has to lug me around.

FEE. Stretch it like I told you.

RONNIE. Yeah.

FEE. You know, if I reminded you of everything I've ever done for you –

RONNIE. No.

FEE. – and then got on my knees and begged you to use the walking stick they made you…

RONNIE. Fee.

FEE. Everyone can see how it hurts.

RONNIE. Then they're taking the right lesson.

FEE. Where do you put it when you're fucking?

RONNIE. Don't feel it when I'm fucking.

FEE. You're lying.

RONNIE. That's another reason.

FEE. So I can tell little Shirley two days?

RONNIE. Short of another war.

FEE. Can I tell her two days?

RONNIE. Yeah, Fee.

(The kitchen door opens and **SHARP** *and* **WILKIE**
enter, pushing two hooded people ahead of them, a
man and a woman.)

WILKIE. My Governor, my Governor, my one and only
Governor, these are for you.

RONNIE. The fuck is this?

SHARP. Sorry. Precaution.

(They force the hooded figures to kneel.)

RONNIE. Precaution against what?

SHARP. We lied a bit.

RONNIE. I'm listening.

WILKIE. You had Shitmouth in here strutting up and
down –

RONNIE. Shitmouth's the Manager of Coral Settlement.
I appointed him. You can call him Manager or Mr.
Smith.

WILKIE. You appointed that guy?

RONNIE. What did you lie about, Sharp?

SHARP. I said "Skins." Only one's a Skin. This one.

(He removes the hood from the woman to reveal
CLARET, *who looks terrified.)*

CLARET. I'm not a Skin.

RONNIE. Is she?

SHARP. Skin or Nampas, one of the two. I think Skin.

RONNIE. Why?

SHARP. Way she uses her body. She's far along, no doubt,
but –

WILKIE. Not like those Twitches you find in the woods with
the shit drying on their legs 'cause they don't have
sense to wipe it off, but still…

SHARP. It's *new*, that's what it is. The body. Every time she
moves a finger it's like it's a miracle.

CLARET. I'm not a Skin, please.

RONNIE. *(to* **SHARP***)* But why either Skin or Nampas?

FEE. *(staring at the hooded man)* Wait a minute…

SHARP. 'Cause nobody but a Skin or a Nampas would be with this guy.

WILKIE. Me 'n' Sharp have been with you how long?

SHARP. You go back to Cubano. Second battle of the War.

WILKIE. We found you in the hills with those crazy fuckers, eating snakes.

SHARP. *(to **RONNIE**)* Point is, we were senior men, so you always gave us the hardest job:

WILKIE. Guarding the man wanted dead by more people than anybody else in the world –

> *(He removes the hood to reveal **ABBIE**.)*

– Mr. Abbie Cooke.

FEE. Oh my god.

RONNIE. *(rising from her chair)* Step away from him.

> **(SHARP** *and* **WILKIE** *step back.* **RONNIE** *walks toward* **ABBIE**.*)*

ABBIE. What happened to your leg?

SHARP. We stand at your pleasure, Governor. For any order. *(pause)*

FEE. If you'd run him through lockup…

SHARP. Folks around here remember him.

WILKIE. I'm not afraid of a bug the size of a house, but I'm afraid of every gramma in this town who lost babies to this traitor and his fucking friends.

SHARP. They'd tear him to pieces. Tear us to pieces if we got in between.

ABBIE. *(looking around him)* We're *here*? This is still *here*?

RONNIE. *(to **SHARP**)* Which way were they going?

SHARP. Northwest.

ABBIE. Fee?

FEE. Go to hell.

RONNIE. Just running or somewhere in particular?

SHARP. Couldn't tell.

RONNIE. Northwest.

ABBIE. *(to* **RONNIE***)* Eight years ago you promised someone you'd keep me safe. Now you can break that promise any number of ways, but there's only one way to keep it.

WILKIE. *(to* **RONNIE***)* Are we letting him talk?

ABBIE. You have to get me out of town before sunrise, before anyone knows I'm here. That's what, eight hours? You better think fast.

SHARP. Governor, we'll obey any order you give, you know that.

CLARET. *(to* **ABBIE***)* That's not her, is it?

ABBIE. Shut up.

RONNIE. Who?

CLARET. *(to* **ABBIE***)* I don't understand.

RONNIE. Not who?

CLARET. *(to* **ABBIE***)* What do I do?

ABBIE. Nothing!

RONNIE. *I'm not who?*

CLARET. Ronnie House Four.

> *(Everyone else in the room knows that this was the wrong thing to say.)*

This *is* Coral Settlement, yes? That's where Ronnie House Four lives.

RONNIE. Won't you know her when you see her?

CLARET. Well she has many faces. Or to be more specific, many people take on the mantle of her name. On every farm a Ronnie would come, and always with a different face. But there's only one true Ronnie House Four.

ABBIE. Claret, enough!

RONNIE. Is that right?

CLARET. What? What did I do?

RONNIE. The one true Ronnie House Four.

CLARET. I'm sorry, I'll stop talking.

RONNIE. How will you know her when you meet her?

CLARET. *(to ABBIE)* Don't I have to answer? I'm her prisoner.

ABBIE. *(to RONNIE)* What's the point?

RONNIE. It's a simple question: how will you know her?

CLARET. Well I would have to rely on description.

RONNIE. No kidding. Description?

CLARET. They say she's small, but terrible. A headdress made of Honeycomb antennae. Honeycomb heads hanging on her wall. Honeycomb blood like a crust on her skin.

RONNIE. Is that right? This lady never washes off?

CLARET. Not Honeycomb blood, that's what they say. Not ever.

RONNIE. But wouldn't it just go rancid and she'd breathe it in and die?

CLARET. Oh, that's a wonderful point.

RONNIE. Is that a wonderful point?

CLARET. I suppose since we don't process oxygen in the same manner I didn't consider –

> *(She realizes her mistake too late.)*

RONNIE. When you say "Ronnie House Four," what do you mean?

CLARET. Oh, well, it's a designation, of course. It's a Honeycomb-devised designation that usefully groups humans according to their present domicile.

ABBIE. Okay, this is stupid. Claret, this –

RONNIE. *(to SHARP and WILKIE)* Maybe if he was over there a bit, and not talking.

> *(Over the following, SHARP and WILKIE drag ABBIE to the far wall and, punch him in the solar plexus.)*

CLARET. Well I don't understand, have I misspoken – Oh! Oh, what are you doing?

RONNIE. It was useful, it was a useful designation.

CLARET. Please don't hurt him anymore!

RONNIE. This here, this house we're in right now, this *domicile*, this was House Four. For about twelve years and change. So anybody who lived in this house, for as long as they were here, they were House Four. Whenever Ronnie was in this house to have her baby, she was Ronnie House Four. When she *had* the baby, the baby went to House One and Ronnie went the whole opposite way down the bank and became Ronnie House Thirty-Eight again. You're right. It *was* useful.

CLARET. This is House Four?

RONNIE. You think that's something, this'll really blow your mind: Before this was a *domicile*, this was a plain old antebuggum human *house*, can you believe that? You're sitting in a museum right now.

CLARET. I feel as though you're angry.

RONNIE. I could take you on a tour, I could show you the rooms upstairs. The one where the mother and father slept. The one where the brother hardly ever slept. The one where the sister never slept. Couldn't preserve original conditions, sorry, got five bug-hunters to a squat up there now, but you could get a sense of what the Cooke residence was like before the bugs made us call it House Four. If I was to take you up there. Which will never fucking happen.

CLARET. By "bugs," do you mean the People of the Honeycomb?

RONNIE. But now that the *bugs* aren't telling us what to call anything, now that this building is the Governor's office of the Coral Settlement Authority, anybody who would still call me Ronnie House Four would have to be one of the bugs.

(**CLARET** *'s whole manner changes.*)

How are you enjoying the body?

CLARET. Forgive me.

RONNIE. *(kneeling beside* **CLARET***)* What's your name? Sorry: what was the name of the person who used to live here?

FEE. *(to* **RONNIE.***)* Ronnie, your leg, you can't go down like that –

CLARET. Claret.

RONNIE. *(touching* **CLARET***'s face)* It's neat, right, Claret? All those nerve endings?

CLARET. Oh, please, please forgive me.

RONNIE. All the tingly places? Have you found 'em all yet?

CLARET. I didn't know, I didn't know…

RONNIE. You know one spot they don't tell you about? Skin lovers like Abbie? They go straight between your legs every time and they never stop to tell you how much you can feel in your ears.

> *(***RONNIE*** gently takes* **CLARET***'s earlobe in her fingers.)*

ABBIE. *(getting his breath back)* Ronnie, look at her, there's no point.

WILKIE. Shut the fuck up.

RONNIE. You feel that? Intense, right?

CLARET. I don't know what I said but I take it back, I take it back a thousand times –

RONNIE. Man knows what to do with your ears you *never* let him go.

CLARET. I beg you.

WILKIE. *(touching his ear)* Huh.

RONNIE. Now you add a little bit of fingernail, just a little bit –

> *(***CLARET*** winces.)*

Yeah? You notice that?

> *(She does it again.)*

You feel that? It's okay if you wanna cry, it's a big feeling, it's new.

CLARET. Oh please.

RONNIE. But I'm being rude, I didn't answer your question.

CLARET. Please.

RONNIE. The answer is, when I say "bugs," I don't mean "People of the Honeycomb," I mean *fucking bugs!*

> *(She twists* CLARET*'s ear, hard.* CLARET *screams.)*

ABBIE. Ronnie! Goddammit, Ronnie, stop!

RONNIE. *(to* CLARET*)* And if you want to talk to *me?* If you want *my* attention? Try to remember this: *My name is Ronnie Cooke!*

> *(She releases* CLARET, *who lies on the floor, weeping.)*

ABBIE. Ronnie, she understands.

RONNIE. *(addressing* ABBIE *for the first time)* I thought you were *dead!*

> *(She tries to rise but her leg locks up.)*

God*dammit!*

FEE. *(going to her)* All right, all right, shut up.

> *(*SHARP *and* WILKIE *are headed for her as well.)*

RONNIE. Oh, goddammit!

FEE. *(to* SHARP *and* WILKIE*)* I got this. *(to* RONNIE*)* Okay, we're gonna take it a bit at a time.

> *(*ZANDER *enters.)*

ZANDER. Governor…are you hurt?

RONNIE. What the fuck are you doing here?

> *(*ZANDER *stares at* ABBIE.*)*

ZANDER. *(to* ABBIE*)* I know you, don't I?

RONNIE. *(to* FEE*)* Come on!

FEE. Come on? This is your fault.

ZANDER. *(to* ABBIE*)* Yes. I know you. I've seen you strapped to the back of a flyer. That was unusual, they didn't make a habit of flying humans around, even top Nampas, so when they made an exception, you always looked really hard at the person's face, trying to guess why.

>(**SHARP** *and* **WILKIE** *flank* **ZANDER***, ready to draw their weapons. They look to* **RONNIE***. At some point over the following she waves them off.*)

ABBIE. I'm who you think I am.

ZANDER. *(to* **RONNIE***)* I left my notes behind. My plan was to ignore whatever I found happening here.

RONNIE. You still could.

ZANDER. *(to* **ABBIE***)* Hello, Abbie Cooke. My name's Zander Smith, formerly Zander House Twenty-Two. It's okay if you don't remember me. I would have been one of a number of skinny young men picking vegetables in the former Coral Farm. I wouldn't have stood out in any way.

ABBIE. All right.

ZANDER. The problem is I stand out now. I'm the Manager of Coral Settlement. People know who I am.

ABBIE. So?

ZANDER. People also know I did nothing of any note in the war. People respect me in this settlement, but only because I've organized it, impeccably, for years. That respect can disappear in an instant. I only have to fuck up once.

ABBIE. *(to* **RONNIE***)* Why is he telling me this?

ZANDER. If the people of this settlement were to learn tomorrow morning that Abbie Cooke, the world's greatest living war criminal, was in our grasp, and that I saw him, and turned a blind eye and allowed his sister to spirit him away like she did so many times during the war – without submission to the process of justice – I'd be finished. They wouldn't blame your sister, that's what's amazing, they would blame *me*. They wouldn't let me shovel gator shit. I'd just have to walk out into the night with the shirt on my back.

RONNIE. Zander: I get it.

ZANDER. *(to* **SHARP** *and* **WILKIE***)* Where was he found?

>(*They look at* **RONNIE***. She nods.*)

SHARP. North mangroves. Headed northwest.

ABBIE. Does that ever get old, Mr. Smith?

ZANDER. What's that?

ABBIE. Everyone looking at Ronnie for permission before they'll so much as answer a question?

ZANDER. Mr. Cooke, any differences I have with the Governor shrink to insignificance compared to those I have with you. *(to* **RONNIE***)* Maybe we should find somewhere to speak.

RONNIE. Northwest...

ZANDER. What?

RONNIE. *(to* **SHARP***)* They were headed northwest?

SHARP. *(to* **WILKIE***)* Tell me if I'm wrong.

WILKIE. About directions? You're never wrong.

ZANDER. But there's nothing northwest. Not for weeks. Am I wrong about that?

WILKIE. Few dozen Nampas hid out that way, but we cleaned them out, shit, forever ago.

RONNIE. Everglades.

CLARET. Abbie!

(**ABBIE** *sharply indicates for her to be quiet.*)

RONNIE. Yeah, that's a live one.

SHARP. What're you thinking?

RONNIE. Remember back when only bits of the world were swamp?

SHARP. Rings a bell.

RONNIE. Those were the places my dad hid the bug eggs in the Time Before.

FEE. But they hatched, right? There's nothing there now.

RONNIE. That's what I *thought*. But it is northwest. Boys?

WILKIE. We stand at your pleasure, day and night.

SHARP. Pick up the trail?

RONNIE. I know you only just got back.

SHARP. Oh, now you're mistaking us for some crybabies in your employ.

RONNIE. Am I?

SHARP. *(tossing a cloak to* **WILKIE***)* Tired?

> *(Over the following* **SHARP** *and* **WILKIE** *re-don bughunter cloaks, get reapers, and get ready to go hunting.)*

WILKIE. Not these feet.

SHARP. I said tired?

WILKIE. Not these hands.

SHARP. I said tired?

WILKIE. Not these arms, not these knees, and not these eyes.

SHARP. Lure 'em down?

WILKIE. Then under the chin!

SHARP. Didn't catch that. Lure 'em down?

WILKIE. Then under the chin!

SHARP. *(to* **RONNIE***)* We're the Governor's guys. Naps are for some other guys. If it's out there?

WILKIE. *(to* **RONNIE***)* It'll be back here.

RONNIE. *Love* it.

SHARP. Send somebody in?

RONNIE. No, tell the POs to look sharp, but *stay* outside.

WILKIE. *(looking at* **ABBIE** *and* **ZANDER***)* You'll be all right?

RONNIE. Come on.

WILKIE. All right then.

RONNIE. Good hunting.

SHARP. Only kind.

WILKIE. Only kind.

> *(They exit.)*

RONNIE. *(to* **ABBIE***)* Probably they won't find anything.

> *(***ABBIE** *looks hard at* **CLARET***, who seems desperate to say something.)*

RONNIE. Sorry, Zander, you were being reasonable?

ZANDER. You don't want to find somewhere private?

RONNIE. Why?

   (beat)

ZANDER. You made a famous promise.

RONNIE. A long time ago.

ZANDER. You understand where you've put me. I've got nothing to lose. If I think you're gonna let him walk I have to get in a longboat and start banging on doors.

ABBIE. You should do that.

ZANDER. What?

ABBIE. Bang on doors. Tie me to a post and wake up the town. I'm sure your legal system can tolerate one exception, right? It's not like mob rule's ever been habit-forming. It's not like you're holding this settlement together with string and my sister's reputation. Wake them up and let them kill me. I'm sure you can calm everyone down right afterwards.

ZANDER. *(to* **RONNIE***)* He's disgusting. But he's right.

RONNIE. Then you better think of something. Sun comes up, someone looks in the window, they'll pull this house down with their hands to get to him.

ZANDER. All right.

   *(***RONNIE*** produces a knife.)*

RONNIE. You wanna be a hero?

   (She holds out the knife to **ZANDER***.)*

Get it done, wipe it off, I'll do the Skin.

ZANDER. All right, Governor.

RONNIE. Man of your age, not one kill to your name. This could be the night.

ZANDER. Yes, Governor, thank you!

RONNIE. *(putting her knife away)* So tell me your better idea.

ZANDER. We have to do this right. We're not at war anymore, we have a process for prisoners now.

RONNIE. Everybody's gone home!

CLARET. What process?

RONNIE. *(indicating* **ABBIE***)* For *Abbie.* We don't have a process for you, you're an animal.

ZANDER. I'm saying, you and I, we have the discretionary power to conduct a trial with no other justices present. We just got through doing it with Budeen.

RONNIE. Provided a defender is present.

ZANDER. Provided a defender is present.

RONNIE. We haven't done a midnight trial since the war.

ZANDER. There's nothing in the law that specifies the time of day.

RONNIE. So everybody wakes up tomorrow...

ZANDER. And justice is done. The process is intact, we can still say every human gets a hearing, and to top it off we have *Abbie Cooke's* body to throw at their feet. We'll be heroes, we'll be able to push through anything we want for months. But Governor, you've got to know, there's no way he walks out of this settlement alive.

RONNIE. Yep.

ZANDER. So we need a defender.

RONNIE. You know who's probably still up?

(They look at each other.)

ZANDER. Oh no. Oh god.

RONNIE. Superior little snot. "No one has to stand up and answer alone." Bring her in here and tell her she's speaking for Abbie Cooke.

ZANDER. I know where she lives.

RONNIE. Be quiet about it.

ZANDER. Of course.

(He's headed for the door when **ABBIE** *speaks.)*

ABBIE. What's the charge?

ZANDER. What did you say?

ABBIE. The charge. Which of your laws will you say I broke?

ZANDER. Well, murder, I imagine, to start.

ABBIE. I've never killed anyone. *(beat)* That's right, Manager, it seems like we have more in common than getting pushed around by my sister.

ZANDER. Treason. Our law specifies, treason against Coral Settlement –

ABBIE. There was no Coral Settlement when I did what I did. It wasn't a sovereign state. I can't commit treason against something that doesn't exist.

ZANDER. All right, obviously we'll need to deliberate, but I can promise you, you are not –

ABBIE. I didn't commit murder, I didn't commit treason, so unless you have a law against genocide you have let me go. Do you have a law against genocide?

ZANDER. It hasn't really come up.

ABBIE. Then you have to let me go. Are you a civilization or not?

RONNIE. So you can keep running northwest.

ABBIE. Or wherever.

ZANDER. Governor, should we find somewhere to talk…

ABBIE. No, you don't need to talk, you need to let me go.

RONNIE. Because you're so fucking smart.

ABBIE. Are you a civilization or not?

RONNIE. You're such a smart little kid.

ABBIE. I asked you a question.

FEE. *(to ABBIE)* You think this is *funny*? *All* of my babies died! Every one of them! You wanna smirk at me too? *(pause)*

ZANDER. Of course we *could* have a law against genocide. Governor, you and I also – provided we both agree – have the discretion to add a law to the code even in the absence of the other Justices of the Council.

RONNIE. Get the book.

> *(**ZANDER** goes to one part of the room and produces a very large, very thumbed sketching pad.)*

ABBIE. Are you serious?

ZANDER. I'll try a draft.

ABBIE. This is really how you do things?

ZANDER. *(flipping to a blank page)* "Resolved that…" or "By joint decree…"

ABBIE. Wait, is that a sketch pad?

RONNIE. What, does it take you back?

ABBIE. That's what you're digging up Miami for? School supplies?

RONNIE. Have you been watching us?

ABBIE. *(going to a shelf of pre-Honeycomb items)* Gotta to keep your nostalgia wall stocked, I guess.

ZANDER. Just a minute more.

ABBIE. Where did you find the radio?

RONNIE. Radio actually works.

ABBIE. Some Nampas I stayed with captured one. That was fun, sitting up nights, listening to people yelling through static, "Have you met Ronnie? What was she like?" until the batteries ran out.

RONNIE. Never thought about captured radios. Is that how you figured out about the bugwater?

ABBIE. Not soon enough.

ZANDER. *(writing)* Or "*attempted*"…

ABBIE. Is that a thermos?

RONNIE. When did you last say that word?

ABBIE. Can I see it?

RONNIE. No.

ABBIE. Why not?

(RONNIE takes a smart phone from the display.)

RONNIE. You can see this.

ABBIE. I can see the phone but not the thermos?

RONNIE. Take it. I want you to.

ABBIE. Got internet on there?

RONNIE. You wanna check your email?

ABBIE. It is probably piling up.

(For a split second they're enjoying each other.)

ZANDER. How about this: "Resolved, by joint decree of Governor Cooke and Settlement Manager Smith, that the extermination or *attempted* extermination of an entire race is prohibited in Coral Settlement, and is punishable by death in every instance of a guilty finding.

RONNIE. Yeah, all right.

ZANDER. We both have to endorse.

RONNIE. Yeah.

ZANDER. Governor: if we both endorse, that's it.

RONNIE. How many times do you think you need to explain this to me?

ZANDER. Yes, Governor.

> *(He makes his mark and then slides it over to* **RONNIE.** *She carefully crosses to* **ZANDER**'s *desk and makes her mark.)*

ZANDER. Abbie Cooke. By my authority as Manager of Coral Settlement, I am detaining you under the charge of attempted genocide. An advocate will be provided for your defense, and provision will be made for you to answer the charges as presented. Do you understand what I've explained to you?

ABBIE. *(to* **RONNIE,** *studying the phone)* It does take me back. I'll give you that much.

ZANDER. Mr. Cooke!

ABBIE. I understand.

RONNIE. *(to* **FEE,** *indicating the sketchpad)* Get it.

FEE. I run errands for you now?

RONNIE. Or you can watch me get it.

> *(**FEE** throws up her hands and exits up the stairs.)*

ABBIE. Get what?

RONNIE. *(to* **ZANDER***)* Better get moving.

ZANDER. What about the Skin?

RONNIE. After we're done here we'll have our guys in the Room shake out whatever she's got.

ZANDER. Should I send some POs in?

RONNIE. I don't want anyone seeing him.

ZANDER. I meant for your safety.

RONNIE. *(to* **CLARET***)* Hey there!

>   (**CLARET** *cowers, covering her head. To* **ZANDER***)*

I'm safe.

ZANDER. I won't be long.

>   (**ZANDER** *exits out the front door. Beat.)*

RONNIE. So.

ABBIE. Yeah.

RONNIE. It's been, what?

ABBIE. Five years? More?

RONNIE. Close to six.

ABBIE. I haven't had any way of keeping track.

RONNIE. Been sleeping rough the whole time?

ABBIE. Running, mostly.

RONNIE. That's what I figured.

ABBIE. I thought, if I could beat you to even one farm.

RONNIE. Stayed up nights scared you would.

ABBIE. If I could warn just one nest they could put out the call.

RONNIE. Would've been all over.

ABBIE. How did you know it takes a whole nest to reach the global Honeycomb?

RONNIE. How do you think?

ABBIE. Conor.

RONNIE. There it is. *(beat)*

ABBIE. I tried going the opposite direction of where you were headed, but still, every farm, the nest was on fire and everyone was talking about Ronnie, Ronnie. How could she be everywhere I go? 'Til one day someone points out a woman I've never seen before and says, "That's her. That's Ronnie."

RONNIE. They were talking about me on the radio. I couldn't be everywhere at once.

ABBIE. So you told your recruiters...

RONNIE. "Tell people your name is Ronnie." People like to have a name.

ABBIE. A nest would go down, we'd guard the next one even tighter...

RONNIE. Doesn't matter how tight if you're looking the wrong way. Looking for an army to come out of the trees instead of your own people you've known for years.

ABBIE. Because who thinks twice about a bottle of water? Especially a race still trying to teach itself the concept of betrayal.

RONNIE. Well, you and Dad were right there if they needed pointers.

ABBIE. Boy, this didn't take long, did it?

RONNIE. Or you could try shutting up.

ABBIE. You know you weren't the only one, right? Folks all over the world figured out about the bugwater. Even we did, after it was too late. They've built this stupid myth around you, but you're not the only one.

RONNIE. I'm the only one who knew how to use it right. I'm the only one who had Conor.

CLARET. We would have worked with you, Ronnie, we still would –

(**RONNIE** *looks at her.*)

I'm sorry, I'm sorry.

RONNIE. *(to* **ABBIE***)* What is she, an Ambassador?

CLARET. Zoologist.

ABBIE. *Anthropologist.*

CLARET. Yes! Right! Anthropologist!

RONNIE. Well, which?

CLARET. I study humans.

RONNIE. You study humans.

CLARET. I observe, I never hurt anyone, I only observe – please don't hurt me, Ronnie Cooke.

RONNIE. *(to* **ABBIE***)* Where'd you find this one?

ABBIE. Leave her alone.

RONNIE. "Leave her alone," maybe I'll leave you both alone, how 'bout that?

ABBIE. Sounds great.

> (**RONNIE** *walks away;* **ABBIE** *looks around the room.*)

God. Benches, knick-knacks... Mom would've hated this.

RONNIE. She might've liked that it's mine.

ABBIE. Electric lights.

RONNIE. Diesel generator, mostly. Some vinegar batteries, potato batteries...

ABBIE. No, it's totally impressive, it's just...

RONNIE. What?

ABBIE. Why didn't you put your office in some other house?

RONNIE. Got used to it.

ABBIE. You couldn't stand being here in the Time Before. You snuck out like every night.

RONNIE. Things changed.

ABBIE. What happened to your leg?

RONNIE. Any of the hundreds of things that can happen to a leg in a war. The fuck do you care which one?

ABBIE. Why don't you have a walking stick?

RONNIE. Because they would fucking love it. I can't get you out of this.

ABBIE. All right.

RONNIE. And I don't want to.

> (**FEE** *enters from the stairs with a box.*)

FEE. Sorry, Ronnie, it was under a lot of shit.

ABBIE. Wait – is that...?

RONNIE. *(to* **FEE***)* You can give it to him.

FEE. I won't.

> (**RONNIE** *takes the drawings from* **FEE** *and gives them to* **ABBIE.**)

RONNIE. Your drawings. Have a little nostalgia before you die.

CLARET. You draw?

ABBIE. No. A long time ago.

CLARET. Let me see!

> (*As* **ABBIE** *and* **CLARET** *look through the drawings,* **RONNIE** *goes to* **FEE.**)

FEE. Let's get you in your chair.

RONNIE. In a second.

> (*She pulls* **FEE** *into a fierce embrace.*)

FEE. They didn't even grow up to be heroes.

RONNIE. You know they would've been.

ABBIE. The Bald Woman.

RONNIE. What?

> (**ABBIE** *holds up a drawing.*)

ABBIE. Remember this? The Bald Woman?

RONNIE. I haven't looked at that shit in years.

ABBIE. But you remember, right? "I saw the Bald Woman. She's on the porch."

RONNIE. Look at your shit and shut up. It's almost over.

ABBIE. *(meaning* **CLARET***)* What about her?

RONNIE. You know what.

ABBIE. Pull out her fingernails 'til she gives up a couple Nampas then throw her to the gators?

RONNIE. Or just the second one. These days gator feed's more valuable than intelligence.

ABBIE. And it doesn't complicate things that she's carrying my child?

CLARET. Abbie!

> (**ZANDER** *and* **TANYA** *enter.*)

ZANDER. *(indicating* **ABBIE***)* Right there.

TANYA. Yes.

ZANDER. You're old enough to remember him?

TANYA. Just barely.

FEE. *(referring to what they heard about* **CLARET***)* Ronnie?

RONNIE. *(low)* Not now, leave it.

ZANDER. Let's be clear, though: you're taking a risk. This will all come out tomorrow. Maybe when we throw his body in the Common everything will be forgotten in the rejoicing, but there's a chance, when people find out you defended Abbie Cooke, that it could come back on you.

TANYA. Let me see the new law.

*(***ZANDER*** goes to get the pad.)*

ZANDER. We'll back you, Ronnie and I will back you, but still –

TANYA. I'd like a minute, please.

(She carefully reads the pad.)

RONNIE. Jesus sake, it's not ten words.

TANYA. I have a condition.

RONNIE. Excuse me?

TANYA. I'm coming in blind, I haven't interviewed the accused, I'm not prepared in any way. And I assume I can't call any witnesses outside this room?

ZANDER. Definitely not.

TANYA. So I need to be able to question him at length. Any questions I want. I need total latitude.

RONNIE. You don't give me conditions.

TANYA. Or I don't have to do it. And you can wake up someone else, tell them Abbie Cooke is here, and ask them to do it.

RONNIE. What is your thing with me?

TANYA. I could ask you that as well, Governor, but I'd rather ask interesting questions.

(beat)

RONNIE. Sun's up in eight hours. This needs to be over by then.

TANYA. I agree.

RONNIE. Well, great. You agree. Set it up.

> *(Over the following, **RONNIE** returns to her main chair and **ZANDER** sets up a chair for **ABBIE**.)*

ZANDER. *(to **ABBIE**)* You'll sit here for questioning.

ABBIE. All right.

TANYA. *(to **CLARET**)* Why don't you come sit with me?

CLARET. Abbie.

ABBIE. It's all right.

CLARET. You must be gentle.

ABBIE. I will be.

ZANDER. *(to **FEE**)* Ms. Holmes, it would confer some legitimacy on these proceedings if you could take notes.

RONNIE. *(to **FEE**)* Fuck that, get some sleep.

FEE. Fuck *that*, I'm not missing this. *(She prepares to take notes.)*

ZANDER. Mr. Cooke, we're going to go straight into it. I'm sure you understand.

ABBIE. I'm ready.

ZANDER. This proceeding is Coral Settlement's prosecution of Abbie Cooke for the crime of attempted genocide against the human race. Settlement Manager Zander Smith speaks for Coral Settlement, Tanya Miller speaks for the accused. Governor Veronica Cooke presides. Sir, can you confirm you are in fact Abbie Cooke?

ABBIE. Yes, I'm Abbie Cooke.

ZANDER. Mr. Cooke, do you promise that every statement you make today will be true on your honor?

ABBIE. Yes.

ZANDER. Mr. Cooke, is it correct that you are the son of William Cooke, the man who brokered the original deal with the Honeycomb to invade and occupy the Earth?

ABBIE. Yes I am.

ZANDER. And in the wake of the Honeycomb invasion, you assisted your father in his work as a representative of the Honeycomb to the human race?

ABBIE. Yes, that's right.

ZANDER. Tell me how you assisted him.

ABBIE. The Honeycomb initially housed humans in crude enclosures while they began the initial phase of terraforming the Earth. I traveled to these enclosures with my father and the other astronauts to explain to the human survivors the new system under which life on Earth would operate.

ZANDER. Meaning slavery.

ABBIE. I know that's the word used by human propagandists.

ZANDER. What is your preferred word for compulsory, uncompensated daily labor?

ABBIE. What do you think the Honeycomb was doing all day? Reclining on sofas? They worked too, *twice* as many hours as you did!

ZANDER. With bodies that are ten times as strong and need almost no sleep.

ABBIE. Bodies that – You know what, we don't have to have this argument anymore. You won.

ZANDER. Is it also true to say that around this same time you formed a close relationship with a member of the Honeycomb named Conor Wells?

ABBIE. He wasn't "named" Conor Wells, he wasn't named anything. He was a Honeycomb consciousness inside the body of a human named Conor Wells.

ZANDER. Ah – "A Honeycomb consciousness inside the body of a human." And how did this Honeycomb consciousness come to be inside this human body?

ABBIE. When my father and his crew first met the People of the Honeycomb on Mars, they couldn't speak to each other; humans aren't telepathic. It was their Ambassador's idea to attempt a telepathic link with the human Conor's mind.

ZANDER. But it didn't work.

ABBIE. No, it did, briefly, long enough for the human Conor to translate the Honeycomb's offer to my father and his crew. But then the telepathic link broke down.

ZANDER. And the result?

ABBIE. The Ambassador's brain superseded and destroyed Conor's. Without a brain, the insectoid body died, and Ambassador was forced to live the remainder of his days in Conor's human body.

ZANDER. Must have been a shock.

ABBIE. He was lost, for a long time. When my father brought him back to Earth, he told everyone Conor had suffered a stroke and lost his memory and motor skills.

ZANDER. And subsequently brought him to live with you and your family. In the house we're standing in right now.

ABBIE. Yes.

ZANDER. And how old were you at this time?

ABBIE. Thirteen.

TANYA. Excuse me – I'm sorry: *This* was the house you grew up in? With Governor Cooke?

ABBIE. We didn't call her Governor Cooke back then.

TANYA. *(to ZANDER)* Did you know this?

ZANDER. *Obviously* I knew it, Ms. Miller. If I can continue?

TANYA. Of course.

ZANDER. So Mr. Cooke, when you found out that Conor Wells was actually an alien life form in a human body, how did you react?

ABBIE. How did I react?

ZANDER. How did you *feel*?

> (TANYA *picks up on it, shoots* ZANDER *a look.*)

ABBIE. I felt like… I always knew. I looked at him and thought, "Of course."

ZANDER. And after the Honeycomb occupied the Earth, you and Conor Wells started a romantic relationship. Is that right?

ABBIE. After?

ZANDER. Or did it start before?

(**ABBIE** *genuinely thinks about it.*)

ABBIE. You know… I met Conor before the Mars mission, I met Dad's whole crew, they came over a lot. To me they were just a blur, boring grownups, indistinguishable. But when Conor came back from Mars – when Dad brought him in the house and said "Conor's gonna live with us now"…I looked at him and he looked at me…

ZANDER. Mr. Cooke?

ABBIE. We always loved each other. From the first minute. Immediately. Never stopped.

ZANDER. Never stopped until he died giving up his body to topple the Coral Farm Honeycomb.

ABBIE. Yeah.

ZANDER. By which time he had defected from the Honeycomb to join the human resistance.

ABBIE. Yeah.

ZANDER. Just wanted to make sure that was clear.

RONNIE. Keep it moving.

ZANDER. So now this process, that put the Ambassador's mind inside Conor's body:

ABBIE. It wasn't a process, it was a mistake.

ZANDER. Well, it was a mistake that *became* a process, right?

ABBIE. The Honeycomb discovered that the transition could be repeated.

ZANDER. And each time the result was the same, right? The insectoid body dies, the human mind dies, but the human *body* stays alive with a Honeycomb consciousness inside, suffering and disoriented, requiring months or years of training to walk or speak, is that right?

ABBIE. And cut off from the voices of its people. Utterly, horribly alone in a way no human being has the context to imagine.

ZANDER. Well, that's what I'm saying, Mr. Cooke: Why repeat the experiment? If the result was so traumatic, why not simply stop with Conor?

ABBIE. We began to see other applications.

ZANDER. Applications, including putting spies inside human homes to root out resistance fighters?

ABBIE. Not just that, we were also building a common gesture language between humans and Honeycomb to open new paths of communication –

ZANDER. But also to spy.

ABBIE. Sure.

ZANDER. And there was one other application you "began to see," correct? What was that one?

ABBIE. Why don't you ask the Governor?

ZANDER. The Governor?

ABBIE. Why don't you ask the Governor, and all the people like her in every settlement in the world, the ones who led murdering parties every night, to kill Honeycomb and human alike. The ones who ensured that all of us, Honeycomb and human, lived out our days in never-ending terror. Why don't you ask her why we might have thought of another reason to put Honeycomb minds in human bodies?

ZANDER. But the question isn't "why," Mr. Cooke. The question is "what." What was the other reason?

ABBIE. Peace. Peace at long last between Honeycomb and human.

ZANDER. Peace achieved how?

ABBIE. By putting every living human through the process of transition.

ZANDER. To put a Honeycomb consciousness inside the body of every living human in the world.

ABBIE. Every one.

ZANDER. But the world's a big place, right? You'd have to start somewhere. Where was this global process of transition going to begin?

ABBIE. Well, obviously you already know the answer, so I don't see –

ZANDER. I know the answers to a lot of these questions. I'm asking anyway.

ABBIE. Right here. Coral Farm. Coral Farm would be first.

ZANDER. Coral Farm. Right here. Where the process of annihilating every human mind on Earth would begin.

ABBIE. While saving every human body.

ZANDER. A worldwide massacre.

ABBIE. A worldwide improvement. A worldwide enhancement of an impoverished, savage race.

CLARET. Gentle, Abbie.

ZANDER. And you, Mr. Cooke, were party to this plan in advance.

ABBIE. I was one of its creators.

ZANDER. You promoted the idea among the Honeycomb.

ABBIE. I pushed it every day. Every time they delayed I pushed them harder. And you know why?

ZANDER. I haven't asked you why.

ABBIE. Because without me they never would have decided to do it. They would have bickered forever inside the Honeycomb, millions of voices arguing millions of points of moral minutiae. It was me who pushed them to act.

ZANDER. And when they did act, Mr. Cooke –

RONNIE. *(to ABBIE)* Seriously?

(Beat. ZANDER is confused but tries to proceed.)

ZANDER. And when they did act, Mr. Cooke –

RONNIE. *(to ABBIE)* You're just gonna skip over the best part?

ABBIE. Who am I talking to?

RONNIE. *(to ZANDER)* Ask him what his part was gonna be in the global Transition.

ABBIE. I'm not hiding it.

ZANDER. Governor, with respect, I have to be able to run my own line of questioning –

RONNIE. Ask him!

ZANDER. Mr. Cooke, what was your –

ABBIE. I volunteered to be first.

ZANDER. First to be transitioned.

ABBIE. That's right.

RONNIE. Ask him why.

ZANDER. Governor, I really must be able to –

ABBIE. You know why.

RONNIE. Do I?

ABBIE. You've known me my whole life. Big useless brain on top of a spindly little body. Why wouldn't I want to be something more than this?

ZANDER. So you volunteered to be first to have your mind replaced by a foreign, alien consciousness.

ABBIE. First to be reborn as a member of the new race.

ZANDER. The new race…in place of the old one.

ABBIE. Meaning?

ZANDER. Meaning, for this new race to be born, the one that already existed had to be expunged, had to be *written over.*

ABBIE. Yes. If that's what it took? For peace? For security? For a thriving, unspoiled ecosystem on this planet? Yes. Absolutely. I just wish I'd made them do it sooner.

ZANDER. Governor, Ms. Miller, I believe I have just elicited a confession from Abbie Cooke, attesting to his central role in a plot to kill the minds of every human being. I offer you, in simpler terms, a man confessing to attempted genocide.

RONNIE. Are you saying you're finished, Manager Smith?

ZANDER. I am, Governor. Thank you. I don't think it gets any plainer than that. Ms. Miller? *(As* **ZANDER** *sits,* **TANYA** *rises.)*

TANYA. Thank you, Mr. Smith. Mr. Cooke, you stated earlier that you and the Governor grew up in this house.

ABBIE. That's right.

TANYA. How far apart were you born?

ABBIE. A little less than two years.

TANYA. You're the younger one, or –?

ABBIE. That's right.

TANYA. Which room did you two sleep in?

ABBIE. We had our own rooms. Second one on the left was mine, all the way at the end was, I guess, the Governor's. *(to* RONNIE*)* Is it still?

TANYA. You had your own rooms?

ABBIE. It's funny, right? Happened a lot in the Time Before. Well, some places, anyway. Of course, there were places all over the world that weren't like that, places that actually didn't change that much when the Honeycomb took over. Seven, eight, nine in a room, kids and grownups. Some of those places barely changed at all, unless you count getting clean water and regular meals for the first time.

RONNIE. None of that sounds like what she asked you.

TANYA. Growing up in two separate rooms, that didn't create a distance between the two of you? As children?

ABBIE. *(studying* TANYA*)* Huh. You're a little different, aren't you?

TANYA. Different from what?

ZANDER. Respectfully, I don't see how we could be any further from the charge under discussion –

TANYA. My arrangement with the Governor is that I may ask the accused any question I like as long as I finish in time for you to kill him before dawn. Now may I get on with it or not?

ABBIE. It didn't create a distance.

TANYA. No?

ABBIE. No, we were…we were close.

TANYA. So, you'd go so far as to say you and Governor Cooke were friends.

ABBIE. That's your question?

TANYA. Please.

ABBIE. You know, under other circumstances I might be a worried about the quality of my representation.

TANYA. But under these circumstances?

ABBIE. I like it. Yes. We were friends. For whatever it's worth now. She looked after me. I couldn't look after myself so she looked after me. We used to... Jesus.

TANYA. What is it?

ABBIE. We used to stay up in *this room* – god, I never thought I'd see this room again. You'd never guess now, but this used to be a room to sit in, and relax. We used to stay up half the night in this room. She'd be venting, you know, someone pissed her off, Mom, Dad, someone at school, I'd be drawing... *(indicating the box of drawings)* Do you mind?

TANYA. Not at all.

ZANDER. Actually we'd prefer that you stay seated for the examination –

> *(But* **ABBIE***'s already gone to the box of drawings and picked it up.)*

ABBIE. *(showing the top drawing.* You see this one?

TANYA. *(taking the drawing from him)* Did you draw that?

ABBIE. *(to* **RONNIE.***)* I saw the Bald Woman, Governor, I swear. When they were bringing me in, I saw her.

RONNIE. That's enough.

ABBIE. She's crawling across the porch right now.

ZANDER. I'm sorry – what's happening?

TANYA. *(meaning the drawing)* What is this?

ABBIE. You all told scary stories when you were kids, right? Or someone told them to you?

TANYA. You're asking me?

RONNIE. She grew up inside a scary story.

ABBIE. So she'd have to invent a new one. Giant insects aren't scary if you see them every day. *(to* **TANYA***.)* That's the Bald Woman. She was our scary story. Thin, hairless, teeth and claws. We used to stay up so late, convincing each other that she was outside on the porch, right there.

TANYA. Do you remember this, Governor? The Bald Woman?

RONNIE. No.

ABBIE. You're kidding, right?

RONNIE. I have no idea what you're talking about.

ABBIE. Then open the door. If she's not out there, crawling on her knees, then open that door.

RONNIE. Ms. Miller, are you controlling this session or not?

ABBIE. It's funny to think about now.

TANYA. What is?

ABBIE. The way we felt about the Bald Woman? That's how the Honeycomb feels about Ronnie. The Nampas, I used to see this all the time, they had a special sign in hands language to show the Honeycomb after a nest burned down. They'd wanna know why, the Nampas would say – *(***ABBIE*** does a hands language sign.)* – "Ronnie House Four was here." It went through the telepathic net like lightning: "Ronnie House Four was here, and now she's coming *there.* The bringer of death is coming there. Tomorrow, or the next day, but she will come, and your nest will burn to the earth." *(to* **RONNIE***.)* In their ten thousand year history, they've never been as scared of anything as they are of you.

TANYA. Mr. Cooke, I need you to focus now.

ABBIE. All right.

TANYA. How long did you and Ronnie remain close?

ABBIE. Right up until.

TANYA. Until the Honeycomb invasion. At which point you chose different sides.

ABBIE. I stood with my father. I believed he was right. Forget "believed," he *was* right.

TANYA. Right about what?

ABBIE. Ah, this sad old shit.

TANYA. I'm sorry?

ABBIE. Saying this sad old shit again.

TANYA. Sad old shit because it's wrong?

ABBIE. Sad old shit because no one ever listens. Sad old shit because every day everyone forgets a little more of it.

TANYA. Forgets what?

ABBIE. Forgets what we were Before. Forgets we sucked sludge out of the Earth and set it on fire to live. Forgets how the bullies hoarded most of everything for themselves, and stomped on anyone who dared to say so. Forgets how every day there were more and more people with nothing, giving birth to more and more people with nothing. Forgets how the folks who lived in *this* part of the world just jerked off all day long while everyone else went without. Forgets how the planet got sicker, hotter, meaner, closer to death, every day.

ZANDER. Ms. Miller, I think we're ready for a new question –

ABBIE. Nobody remembers any of *that*, so everybody's fine to walk around and curse me and curse my father because the very fact that he succeeded meant *no one would ever know he was right*. And I look at them, and I look at *you*, and these days, I swear, I *swear*, I wish he'd failed. I wish he'd given up. I wish he'd let you all just live in hell.

RONNIE. We don't live in hell?

CLARET. Abbie, gentle.

RONNIE. Why the fuck do you care if he's gentle?

TANYA. But Mr. Cooke, what do you make of the fact that so many humans disagreed with you that they gave up their lives in horrible agony to end the Honeycomb occupation?

ABBIE. "Occupation" – they needed a place to live! Everyone needs a place to live! Is that what we are?

"No, go away, go someplace else and die, as long as I don't have to see"?

TANYA. But what do you make of it?

ABBIE. You know what, quit talking like you're unveiling some great mysterious virtue. You're talking about *nothing*. If you spring a gator from a trap, it's still a gator, it won't say thanks, it'll fucking bite you, and that's all you're talking about!

CLARET. That's a metaphor, I know metaphors!

TANYA. What?

CLARET. "We sprang the human race from its trap, but they bit us anyway." I know metaphors. *(to ABBIE)* But you're wrong.

> *(There is suddenly a strange chirping sound in the distance. Everyone immediately goes into a different mode.)*

ZANDER. What's that?

FEE. It's gotta be bound, right?

ZANDER. If it wasn't bound up we'd have heard an out-bell.

RONNIE. Shit, that close, one of the scouts would've seen it days ago.

> *(ABBIE and CLARET are looking at each other. To FEE:)*

You know what it sounds like, right?

FEE. *(to RONNIE, realizing)* No…

ZANDER. *(calling out the front door)* Send a runner! Get eyes on it!

RONNIE. The contingency?

FEE. Filled it up yesterday.

TANYA. Do I continue?

ABBIE. What contingency?

RONNIE. *(to TANYA)* Keep going for now.

TANYA. So Mr. Cooke, given how close you and your sister once were, what was your reaction, when you found out she was operating an insurgency out of the house you grew up in?

ABBIE. I couldn't do anything. The Honeycomb wanted proof – somehow, proof beyond "It couldn't be anyone else." All I could do was try to talk her out of it. You should've seen some of those conversations.

TANYA. I wish I had.

ABBIE. No you don't.

TANYA. Yes, I do. Why didn't you ever try to have her killed?

ABBIE. What?

TANYA. This is what I've never understood. If the Governor was so important to the resistance, why not just kill her?

ZANDER. Ms. Miller, the point of this hearing isn't to help you with what you've "never understood."

TANYA. Don't *you* want to understand? This is *Abbie Cooke*, this is history sitting in a chair! In a couple hours he'll be gator feed! Don't you want to ask every question you possibly can?

ZANDER. No, I don't! Who cares? We have real problems in this Settlement, real, actual problems that require our attention *now*, and we're up all night rehashing the same tired shit?

TANYA. Mr. Cooke, why –

ZANDER. Bill Cooke, Abbie Cooke, Conor Wells – When do we get to stop talking about this?

TANYA. Mr. Cooke, why didn't you have the Governor killed?

ABBIE. What?

TANYA. So many other people were killed. You may not have killed anyone yourself, but you had no problem letting so many other people die.

ABBIE. I had *no problem*?

TANYA. Why didn't you kill Ronnie?

ABBIE. I tried to have her sent away. Savannah Farm.

TANYA. To start another insurgency there?

ABBIE. I guess, probably.

TANYA. So why didn't you kill her? Mr. Cooke. You're gonna die. Within hours. You're not gonna get another chance.

ABBIE. I should have, I just…

TANYA. You should have?

ABBIE. Obviously, *now*, looking back.

TANYA. Obviously?

ABBIE. So many would still be alive today.

TANYA. How could you have known?

ABBIE. I was a weak kid in the Time Before. Other kids saw how much they could hurt me and they just couldn't resist. One time Ronnie caught one of them hurting me, and she…

TANYA. Mr. Cooke?

ABBIE. She beat him so badly he begged her to stop. Blood and snot on his face. He sounded like a baby bird.

TANYA. That really happened?

ZANDER. Ms. Miller *please.*

TANYA. *(to* **RONNIE***)* Did that really happen?

ABBIE. I knew what she was. I knew what she could do. There's no way I could say I didn't.

TANYA. So why didn't you kill her? *(pause)* Mr. Cooke, I'll ask you another question. At the time you made this plan with the Honeycomb, to transition into every human body on Earth:

ABBIE. Right.

TANYA. At that time, was the Honeycomb capable of killing every living human?

ABBIE. Come on.

TANYA. Answer the question. At that time –

ABBIE. Of course! What kind of question is that? They took over the world, back when we had weapons like you couldn't even imagine! It took them a *month!*

TANYA. So you could have stopped the insurgent raids by simply exterminating the human race in, say, a couple of weeks.

ABBIE. That wasn't the deal.

TANYA. You're talking about the deal your father made on Mars.

ABBIE. "Save our people, and we'll save yours."

TANYA. So by choosing this transition process, instead of simply killing us all…

ABBIE. You really put details together, don't you?

TANYA. You believed that you were…partially saving us?

ABBIE. Not just me. The Governor believes it too.

RONNIE. *What?*

TANYA. A moment, Governor – Mr. Cooke –

RONNIE. You piece of shit, what did you say?

TANYA. One moment. *(to* **ABBIE***)* Do you want to clarify that?

ABBIE. Right here, in Coral Settlement, you have a large penal facility housing Transitioned Humans, right? I'm sorry, you probably know them as "Twitches."

RONNIE. You have been watching us.

TANYA. I don't care for that term.

ABBIE. Maybe not, but you still live under the protection of a settlement that stores them like animals, so don't pat yourself on the back.

CLARET. Can you imagine how frightened they are?

ABBIE. People of the Honeycomb: they watched their nest burn and they fled in panic into the nearest human body. No one around to show them how to use it. Lost, weak, uncoordinated, not even a shred of language to beg for help. Stop me when I say something wrong.

ZANDER. There's a difference between *wrong* and *irrelevant.*

ABBIE. *(to* **TANYA***)* Ask her why she houses them. Ask her why she feeds them. She's never hesitated to kill any of the Honeycomb in their insectoid form, obviously, so why does she keep all these alive at what must be colossal effort?

ZANDER. You don't know the half of it…

RONNIE. Okay, you wanna do this?

TANYA. Governor, please, my conditions were clear –

ABBIE. Why do you keep them alive?

RONNIE. You wanna do this?

ABBIE. Because you know they're still human in almost every way! Sensory perception, digestion, *reproduction*, you name it, all still human.

RONNIE. I swear to *god* –

ZANDER. Are we anywhere near some sort of argument?

TANYA. Mr. Cooke, something's just occurred to me.

ABBIE. Yeah, I can see that. Good for you.

TANYA. Reproduction.

ABBIE. You're so close. You're *so* close.

TANYA. Some of the prisoners, the more advanced ones, some of them have had children.

ABBIE. Have you taught them any language, these children? At all?

RONNIE. We feed them out of our fucking crop! Food they don't work for! You think we owe them *language*?

ABBIE. So that means you can't ask them questions.

TANYA. Mr. Cooke, have other Transitioned humans, not, all right, not "Twitches," but fully trained ones, Transitioned back in the occupation…

ABBIE. Have they had children? Yes. Some are as old as nine years.

TANYA. Children of *two* Transitioned parents.

ABBIE. You're almost there.

> (*The chirping sound again.* **FEE** *goes to the window.*)

TANYA. Have these children been taught language?

ABBIE. I've been wondering – for *years* – when one of you would think to ask.

FEE. I can see the runner. Actually – I see the bughunters.

ZANDER. They're already back?

FEE. They're dragging something.

RONNIE. What?

FEE. Can't tell. Still no bells, though. Nobody seems to think it's an attack.

RONNIE. *(to* TANYA*)* You. Last question.

ABBIE. Better make it a good one.

TANYA. Mr. Cooke…

ABBIE. Right.

TANYA. When these children learn to speak, and you ask them what they can remember…

ABBIE. Not one of them remembers the Honeycomb. Never once. Not one kid. Not a single one of them remembers the ten thousand years, the homeworld, all the extraordinary things their forbears made and learned. Every single one of these children is born fully human.

TANYA. So even if you were successful…

ABBIE. You would've survived. Can you fucking believe that? After everything – after *everything* – you miserable people would've survived.

TANYA. Governor Cooke, Mr. Smith, I'm going to request now that the charge of attempted genocide be summarily dismissed.

ZANDER. *What?*

TANYA. I'm going to request –

ZANDER. First of all, if what he's saying is even *true* –

TANYA. May I finish making my request?

RONNIE. Both of you shut up.

ZANDER. Governor – listen – Governor –

(*The chirping sound starts again.*)

RONNIE. I said shut up! What the fuck is happening out there?

(SHARP *and* WILKIE *enter.*)

WILKIE. Ronnie! Governor! You have to see this!

(ZANDER *and* FEE *run to the window.*)

ZANDER. What *is* that?

FEE. Oh my god.

RONNIE. Fee?

FEE. It's...

RONNIE. On my side!

(**FEE** *runs to* **RONNIE** *and helps her up.*)

WILKIE. We tied it up, got some guys to drag it back – don't worry, guys we trust.

SHARP. It was right under our noses. God knows how long.

ZANDER. It's gonna wake up half the Settlement.

RONNIE. Get me there!

(**FEE** *gets* **RONNIE** *to the window.*)

CLARET. *(to* **ABBIE***)* This is it, isn't it?

ABBIE. No.

CLARET. This is the end of everything.

ABBIE. No.

FEE. *(to* **RONNIE***)* It is, isn't it?

RONNIE. It's a Queen. It's a *fucking Queen.*

WILKIE. It was running when we found it, all covered in some kind of slime, dragging those eggs –

SHARP. Governor, I'm so ashamed –

RONNIE. *Eggs?*

WILKIE. Like, thousands of them. Like thousands of them!

RONNIE. How close to hatching?

SHARP. Can't say for sure, but look at 'em. They're full sized.

ZANDER. It's gonna wake up everyone!

RONNIE. *(to* **ABBIE***)* Just running northwest, huh? Just out for a run, nothing special? *(to* **SHARP** *and* **WILKIE***)* Burn it. Get the stuff. Burn her, burn the sac, burn everything.

ABBIE. You can't.

RONNIE. Fuck you.

ABBIE. You can't. Ronnie? Governor? You can't.

RONNIE. Watch me. Stand right here at the window, and watch me.

ABBIE. No, I mean you *can't.* It's against the law.

RONNIE. What?

ABBIE. She's the last one. She's the last Queen. In the whole world. You can't kill her. It's against the law of Coral Settlement. It's genocide.

End of Act One

ACT TWO

*(Before dawn. **ABBIE** and **CLARET** are dozing, sitting up. Periodic shrieks from the Queen outside.)*

CLARET. Abbie?

ABBIE. Go back to sleep.

CLARET. *(indicating the wall of names)* Whose names are those?

ABBIE. I'm not sure. I know a few of them.

CLARET. Conor's up there.

ABBIE. Yeah.

CLARET. Abbie: this isn't going to work.

ABBIE. It has to. Go back to sleep.

> *(**CLARET** rests her head against **ABBIE** and drifts off. After a beat, **RONNIE** and **WILKIE** enter, **WILKIE** supporting **RONNIE** a bit. **RONNIE** moves toward **ABBIE** and **CLARET**, but **WILKIE** stops her.)*

WILKIE. Wait wait wait, hold up a second, don't wake them up yet, c'mere.

RONNIE. What? Oh, Wilkie, seriously.

> *(**ABBIE** opens his eyes and watches them.)*

WILKIE. What? Come on. When are we gonna be alone again, it's gonna be days.

> *(He kisses her. **RONNIE** plays along.)*

My *Governor.*

RONNIE. Thanks, Wilkie.

WILKIE. That was just practice. Thank me for *this.*

> *(He kisses **RONNIE** again, longer this time.)*

WILKIE. How's the leg?

RONNIE. Leg's okay. Leg's fine.

(There is a piteous chirping sound from outside.)

Come on.

WILKIE. Hey, one second, one second. You know I'm the man for you, right?

RONNIE. You're good to me, Wilkie, thank you.

WILKIE. No, I'm saying I'm gonna *keep* being good to you. I'm gonna be the guy who stays. I know there's been a lotta guys – I know there was one main guy way back when – but I'm different. I'm the guy who's gonna stay.

RONNIE. Who told you that?

WILKIE. Told me what?

RONNIE. That there was a main guy way back when.

WILKIE. I don't know.

RONNIE. You don't know?

WILKIE. I guess…everybody just knows.

RONNIE. What do they say about him?

WILKIE. Nothing, just… I don't even know where I heard it. Ronnie – Governor – I'm not trying to upset you.

RONNIE. You don't remember who told you?

WILKIE. I just want you to know that I'm never leaving you. I just want you to know you can count on me.

(Another shriek from the Queen.)

RONNIE. We gotta do this.

*(**WILKIE** crosses to **CLARET** and **ABBIE**, who feigns sleep.)*

WILKIE. Hey, Skin.

ABBIE. What's that?

WILKIE. I need the Skin.

ABBIE. Give her a second, she's waking up.

WILKIE. It's starting to make noise again. We need her to do the hands language, get it to be quiet.

CLARET. No, I have to sleep more.

RONNIE. Hey! Skin! Guess what happens when the whole Settlement wakes up and gets a look at that eggsac!

CLARET. I'm awake, Ronnie Cooke, I'm sorry, I'm awake.

ABBIE. Are you all right?

CLARET. These bodies…

ABBIE. I know.

CLARET. They just need so much sleep!

ABBIE. You'll be all right.

CLARET. How do you live like this, sleeping all the time?

WILKIE. We really gotta get out there.

CLARET. Yes. Yes. I'm following you.

> *(She's following* **WILKIE** *out when* **RONNIE** *stops her.)*

CLARET. Ronnie Cooke?

RONNIE. How long 'til they hatch?

CLARET. I don't know.

RONNIE. How could you not know?

ABBIE. She's telling the truth. We don't know.

RONNIE. Go.

> *(***WILKIE** *gives* **RONNIE** *one last significant look, and then he and* **CLARET** *exit.)*

ABBIE. She needs to rest. She's carrying.

RONNIE. How much rest do you think I got when I was carrying?

ABBIE. And that was a good thing? That others should emulate?

RONNIE. You want that thing to wake up a mob?

ABBIE. A mob's waking up anyway, Ronnie, it's almost dawn. You have to make a decision *now*, you have to decide if this is a settlement of laws or –

RONNIE. You know what? You start that shit as soon as everyone's back. I'll be fucked if I'm gonna listen to it now. *(beat)* How long have you been with her?

ABBIE. How long have you been with him?

RONNIE. All right.

ABBIE. I thought you liked them older.

RONNIE. I thought you liked them male. *(pause)*

ABBIE. I talked more about Conor tonight than I have in years.

RONNIE. If you were one of mine, I'd tell you he died bravely.

ABBIE. You probably got pretty good at that.

RONNIE. I did.

ABBIE. It's the obvious follow-up. First you get them to blow themselves up, then you tell their people they died bravely.

RONNIE. They did.

ABBIE. I guess we could have a big fight about this.

RONNIE. We could.

ABBIE. Why don't you have a walking stick? It's so stupid that you don't have a walking stick.

> *(**RONNIE** gives him a look.)*

All right. Do your thing.

> *(He approaches the wall of names.)*

Now why would Conor's name be just above Peck's?

> *(His hand almost touches Peck's name.)*

RONNIE. Don't touch him.

ABBIE. Now why would there ever be a list with both their names on it?

RONNIE. Well, you were always a smart kid.

ABBIE. They're the ones who took down the first Honeycomb, right? These are the original murderers.

RONNIE. Choose your next words very carefully.

ABBIE. Because if I say "You sent them to their deaths" you'll just say the same thing right back to me. Because this is who we are now. No surprises anymore.

RONNIE. Guess not. *(pause)*

ABBIE. How's his fingerblasting?

RONNIE. What?

ABBIE. That guy. I didn't get his name.

RONNIE. I haven't heard fingerblasting in twenty years.

ABBIE. It's like "thermos" though, right? Pops right back in there.

RONNIE. Too fast some days, too slow the other days.

ABBIE. Oh yeah?

RONNIE. Since you asked.

ABBIE. Some guys don't know what they're doing.

RONNIE. Nope.

ABBIE. Some guys do.

RONNIE. Yeah.

> (**ABBIE** *touches Conor's name.*)

ABBIE. I haven't read letters in so long, you think it would take a minute, but... "Conor."

RONNIE. All right, look:

ABBIE. I was a fucking fool. I was just such a fool.

RONNIE. You know I can't comfort you.

ABBIE. I know.

RONNIE. I'm not kidding.

ABBIE. I know. If they saw you –

RONNIE. It's not that. It's you. I don't have comfort for you.

> (*pause*)

ABBIE. You know what question I keep waiting for but nobody asks?

RONNIE. Forget it.

ABBIE. No one's asked me, "Hey, Abbie, wasn't it you who flipped the switch –"

RONNIE. I said forget it.

ABBIE. "Wasn't it you who flipped the switch that hatched all the Honeycomb eggs in the world? Weren't you the one who turned Before into After?" How come no one's ever asked me that? In twenty years, not once? *(beat)* You never told anyone.

RONNIE. That's not on you. You were a kid. Dad and his people put that switch there. If you hadn't flipped it one of them would.

ABBIE. Well but...really? See this is what I always try to think: 'Cause you had that gun in your hands, right? And you would've killed anyone else in that room who tried to flip that switch. Even Dad, even Mom. Until I walked over to flip it myself. It didn't take me long, like two seconds, but you had the gun on me the whole time and you didn't fire.

> *(***RONNIE*** *has made her way to the reapers and picks one up.)*

RONNIE. Remember these?

ABBIE. Of course.

RONNIE. Reapers. Honeycomb-designed.

ABBIE. For gardening. Subsequently repurposed by your people.

RONNIE. This is what they're gonna use when they kill you.

ABBIE. I don't care what they use.

RONNIE. And I'm not gonna stop them.

ABBIE. I didn't think you would.

RONNIE. Not because I don't have a choice. Because you deserve to die.

ABBIE. Isn't there a part of you that looks at the stairs and thinks any second Dad's gonna clomp down and yell at us for still being up?

RONNIE. No, Abbie.

ABBIE. Do whatever you want to me. Do anything. But please –

RONNIE. Don't. I mean it.

> *(***SHARP*** *enters.)*

SHARP. She's subdued. We got her tied down tight.

RONNIE. She'll be quiet?

SHARP. Skin did something. Hands language. Seems to be working.

RONNIE. Thanks, Sharp.

SHARP. Governor.

RONNIE. What is it, Sharp?

SHARP. Can I take your arm?

> (**SHARP** *leads* **RONNIE** *as far away from* **ABBIE** *as possible.*)

SHARP. I'm gonna turn in my gear. Join a farm crew.

RONNIE. What?

SHARP. I'm disgraced.

RONNIE. Fuck that.

SHARP. Queen? Egg-sac with thousands? Not an hour from your door? It's inexcusable. I'm handing in my gear. Wilkie should too. Up to him.

RONNIE. They had help.

SHARP. A lot of them have help. No excuse.

RONNIE. We don't even know how long it was there.

SHARP. These are my grounds.

RONNIE. I'm not taking your fucking gear. We're not talking about this.

SHARP. I can't look my own guys in the face.

RONNIE. You went back out on my hunch, picked up a dead trail, extrapolated it to its destination, found the thing, bound it, and brought it back in less than an hour. Nobody can do that. You're unique. You think I'd let you walk?

SHARP. I'll do whatever you say.

RONNIE. Sit.

> (*They sit.*)

You're the heart of my team. You're the heart. I won't take your gear.

SHARP. All right.

RONNIE. None of this works without you.

SHARP. All right.

RONNIE. You don't talk much, do you?

SHARP. I'd have to *think* much first, and I don't.

RONNIE. Doesn't stop anyone else. *(She's very close to him by now.)* You tired?

SHARP. I will be later.

RONNIE. You must be exhausted.

SHARP. You trained me.

RONNIE. I remember.

SHARP. Saved my life.

RONNIE. You don't have to say that. It was war, it was fast, I wasn't thinking about being a hero.

SHARP. I'd follow any order from you. I'd put down my life.

RONNIE. I'm not asking you to.

SHARP. But Wilkie's my best friend. *(pause)* So.

RONNIE. All right.

SHARP. I should get back out there.

RONNIE. No, get Wilkie, I want you both in here. It's about to get shitty.

SHARP. Got it.

    (FEE enters as SHARP leaves.)

RONNIE. *(to FEE)* You don't have to be here.

FEE. I checked on her, by the way. She's fine.

RONNIE. You're talking about the Queen?

FEE. …No, Ronnie. I'm talking about little Shirley.

RONNIE. Okay.

FEE. Your daughter. With Peck.

RONNIE. Good, good – so you went by the house – so she's good – good. She wasn't asleep?

FEE. She went back to sleep. She asked for you. I told her tomorrow.

RONNIE. I thought it was two days.

FEE. Not anymore. Now it's tomorrow.

RONNIE. Yeah – yeah. I don't know what I'm…

FEE. *(touching* **RONNIE***)* I *want* to be here.

> *(***ZANDER, TANYA, CLARET, SHARP,*** *and* **WILKIE***
> enter.)*

ZANDER. All right, we have to move fast.

TANYA. We managed to get most people back to bed.

ZANDER. This is insane, we've lost so much time!

RONNIE. Anybody see Abbie?

ZANDER. It's dawn in an hour! Maybe less!

TANYA. *(indicating* **CLARET***)* I don't think so, but some
people saw her using the hands language. They know
we have a full Transitioned in here.

ZANDER. Twice as many problems to solve in a fifth of the
time! How does this happen?

RONNIE. You want my job someday, Zander? This is *all* that
happens.

ZANDER. *(to* **SHARP***)* How did we miss this? How did *you* miss
this?

WILKIE. How 'bout you take a step back?

TANYA. It doesn't matter who missed it, she's here now –

ABBIE. He didn't miss it, we tricked him. *(to* **SHARP***)* You,
you're a – what's your name?

SHARP. You don't worry about my name.

WILKIE. You don't remember us? We only used to be your
fucking bodyguards.

ABBIE. Forget your name, doesn't matter, your job, what do
you call your job?

WILKIE. He's a bug hunter. Just like me. You got something
to say about it?

ABBIE. About a despicable term like "bug hunter"? No,
nothing. How do you track Queens?

RONNIE. *(to* **SHARP***)* Play along.

SHARP. Cluster-hunting.

ABBIE. You work the patterns.

SHARP. Crawlers surround her in four clusters of four but
you can't always see them. You watch for the flyers,

they're above the treeline: three ahead, three behind. Spot them first, then scout the crawlers, then map out the center, and there's your Queen.

ABBIE. Took us most of the war to figure that out.

SHARP. Always wondered about that.

ABBIE. You know what you do is sickening, don't you?

CLARET. We don't have time for this!

ZANDER. Thank you!

ABBIE. We tricked you. Well maybe not you, whatever teams we ran into between here and Savannah. We set up fake clusters going in two directions. You should've seen me trying to persuade them: "No, this is the *good* kind of lying."

RONNIE. We tracked every Queen in Savannah years ago. I was there.

ABBIE. You wouldn't have known to look for her. They weren't guarding her like a Queen.

SHARP. Why not?

CLARET. Because she's old. She's one of the original hatched. She bore her generation. You know how hard it is to bear a second? We thought she was too old to have any more babies.

RONNIE. *(to SHARP and WILKIE)* Guys?

SHARP. It's possible. She's definitely weak.

WILKIE. Maybe sick, not that I know what bug-sick looks like.

CLARET. Think if a human woman of fifty years was carrying triplets.

ABBIE. This is what I've been doing since I got away from you. We stopped trying to win and just tried to survive, which meant getting to the Queens and getting them safe. But you kept getting to them first.

CLARET. There was still a nest in Portland Farm, strong enough to reach the global Honeycomb. We reached our minds across the world, asking, asking, asking, "Have you seen one?" "Where did you see her?" "When you last saw her, was she alive?"

ABBIE. Can you even wrap your shitty little minds around what you've done?

CLARET. The answer came from across the continent in Savannah. "I don't know if I can have any more. But I'll try."

TANYA. I'm having a hard time believing you.

CLARET. It's the truth.

TANYA. If she really is the last of your kind capable of producing offspring, why would you ever take the risk of putting her right next door to Ronnie Cooke?

ABBIE. We didn't want to, believe me.

CLARET. We needed the Everglades.

RONNIE. Fuck. Dad's original site.

CLARET. *(to TANYA)* The Ambassador told her father on Mars how to make the natal fluid the egg-sacs rest in before the hatching. With all the nests burned, our only hope was that there was still a decent quantity left over at each original site.

RONNIE. So you took her to the closest one.

CLARET. We didn't know if she would even survive this far. But she's incredible.

ZANDER. But they're not in the fluid now. Can they still hatch?

CLARET. They should, they're hatching size.

ZANDER. They're *hatching size?*

RONNIE. *When* will they hatch?

CLARET. I don't know.

RONNIE. How can you not know?

FEE. What, like *we* always knew exactly when *we* would hatch?

CLARET. Everything about this is irregular. She's not even supposed to try for another four years. I just don't know.

ZANDER. But it could be tomorrow. Or tonight. Or in ten minutes.

CLARET. I'm sorry.

RONNIE. Wilkie. Get the stuff. Now.

WILKIE. On it, on it, on it.

(WILKIE *exits out the front door.*)

ABBIE. Wait, what is the stuff?

ZANDER. How do we know you're telling the truth?

CLARET. We are!

ZANDER. Yeah, see, that doesn't help.

ABBIE. Ronnie? What's the stuff?

TANYA. *(to CLARET)* You have to think about it from our point of view. It would make sense, tactical sense, to have us believe she's the only one, while dozens of others all over the world –

CLARET. I wish there were dozens of others all over the world, but you killed them! I'm sorry, I'm sorry, but you killed them. I'm sorry. But I've seen it. I've hidden in trees watching bug hunters slashing one egg after another, speculating each time: would they see fluid running out or perhaps a little leg? I'm sorry, but some of you are terrible creatures.

FEE. That's really sad.

CLARET. What?

FEE. That's just so sad. That your babies died.

CLARET. It was sad.

FEE. It must have broken your heart.

CLARET. I know that metaphor! Yes. It did. Thank you.

(CLARET *takes a closer look at* FEE.)

You're not being sincere in some way.

FEE. You think?

TANYA. But you see what I mean? There's no way to prove you're telling the truth.

CLARET. But there is a way. Of course there's a way. You can kill the Queen, and watch what happens thereafter. You will start to notice there are fewer and fewer of us. In the sky, in the trees, on the water. *(to* **SHARP***)* You, and your other hunters, you will go out on your expeditions, and more days than not you will come home with nothing. Perhaps this is already happening?

SHARP. Yeah.

CLARET. And then one day, it will occur to one of you that you haven't seen one of the Honeycomb for a whole season. Then for a year. Then never again. A ten-thousand-year-old civilization.

> *(Over the following,* **TANYA** *goes to the Book of Law and flips to the page on genocide.)*

ZANDER. You understand, don't you, that that doesn't sound entirely disagreeable to a lot of people in this room?

ABBIE. Except that Coral Settlement has a law against genocide.

ZANDER. Yes. Thank you.

ABBIE. It's either bad thing or it's not.

ZANDER. You being the authority, of course.

ABBIE. Even my attempted genocide allowed new humans to be born. Are you gonna be worse than me?

RONNIE. And you knew that would happen when you came up with the plan, right? Or not?

ABBIE. What does it matter what I knew? That was the result.

RONNIE. If we're talking "attempted," what you knew is pretty fucking important!

ZANDER. It makes no difference anyway. What would it matter if the children were born human? You'd still raise them under a hostile alien culture! You'd raise them to be slaves!

ABBIE. We'd raise them to have different values than their ancestors, sure. That's only happened like *hundreds* of times in human history.

CLARET. Abbie why can't you stop? With everything that's at stake why can't you just stop?

TANYA. *(looking at the book)* This is really good, Zander.

ZANDER. What?

TANYA. This is good work. "That the extermination or *attempted* extermination of an entire race" – it's simple, it's clear...you're really good at this.

ZANDER. What are we talking about?

TANYA. Of course you left off the word "human."

ZANDER. I left off – It was fast! I was tired!

TANYA. How do we even finish his trial, knowing the decision we have to make next?

ZANDER. Are you crazy? We're not finishing his trial. What, we're gonna find him not guilty because he didn't pull it off?

TANYA. Is this the law of the land or not?

ZANDER. Fine, let's say *not!* Let's repeal it. Governor, we're gonna repeal it.

TANYA. Then we have to let him go.

ZANDER. No, we're not letting him go!

TANYA. But you hear how you sound, right? Either these laws reflect what we believe or they don't.

RONNIE. The fuck is wrong with you?

ZANDER. What am I saying, we couldn't let him go if we wanted to – they know him out there! The only way he walks out of this house is if the whole entire Settlement is looking in a different direction!

CLARET. Neither of us expects to walk out of this house.

RONNIE. How do you see this ending, Skin? The sun's coming up. My settlement's five thousand strong. Not a one of them came out of the war without losing three, four, five, some even more. They're gonna wake up with the sun like they always do, and it's gonna be pretty fucking hard for them not to notice a giant bug in my yard with a giant goddam egg-sac sticking out of its ass. At which point *anything* you saw in the war is gonna look like child's play. So I don't get why you're acting like this is in our hands at all.

ABBIE. If you had even a shred of decency –

CLARET. Let me do it. Please. *(beat)* Ronnie Cooke. Governor. Do you know how we got to Mars in the first place?

RONNIE. I don't, and I don't care.

TANYA. Some kind of spaceship.

CLARET. We don't have space ships. Our technology's organic. When we need something new, we develop it in our bodies.

RONNIE. How do you go through space without a spaceship?

CLARET. There's a reason the fluid in our thoracic cavity – the bugwater, yes? you say bugwater? – is so volatile. It's something we developed for space travel. The, the fluid, if mixed with short bursts of adrenaline – not exactly adrenaline, our equivalent of adrenaline –

ABBIE. Claret.

CLARET. It's hard to talk to you, Ronnie Cooke!

TANYA. You use controlled explosions of your own bodies to move through space.

> *(**CLARET** looks at **TANYA**.)*

Talk to me.

CLARET. We don't process oxygen like you do. We can store it and draw from it over a long time. When our planet was dying, when all we could do was run, we formed a giant sphere: all the Queens at the center, then the rest of us, in hundreds of airtight layers around them. The outermost layer drew on stored oxygen as long as they could and when there was none left they detonated themselves to propel the sphere or make a course correction.

TANYA. So many must have died on the way.

CLARET. We don't think about our lives the same way you do. We ask ourselves, "What small thing did I do to help build the Honeycomb?"

TANYA. So when *we* drank this same…thoracic fluid…

CLARET. We never thought it would work in an atmosphere. There's something different about your bodies.

TANYA. But what you're saying is, you could do it again.

CLARET. Not me, I'm in this body now, I can't go back. But they could.

ZANDER. Back home.

CLARET. Not home, it's not there anymore, but somewhere.

TANYA. How do you know you'd find a planet this time?

CLARET. We don't.

RONNIE. But in order for *any* of this to happen:

CLARET. You'd have to let us hatch.

RONNIE. Ten, twenty thousand eggs.

CLARET. You'd have to let us hatch.

    (Silence.)

ZANDER. This is…this is… We should have some sort of delegation, we should have Governors from every settlement in the world, as many as we could reach, a decision like this…

RONNIE. Tough shit. It's just us.

ZANDER. The radio. We can raise them on the radio! Let me just –

RONNIE. *And* wake up all the Governors, *and* explain the situation, *and* give them time to wring their hands and throw in their worthless two cents before the sun comes up?

ZANDER. I don't know!

RONNIE. They could hatch any time. They could be hatching right now.

ZANDER. *This is insane!*

CLARET. Ronnie Cooke – Governor – *please.*

TANYA. You would just leave. They would hatch, they would form this sphere, and they would just fly away.

CLARET. Yes! Yes! I swear!

TANYA. Knowing you might not find anywhere to land.

CLARET. I swear!

ABBIE. Or, you know, alternatively, you could look in your heart and find some fucking *mercy*, and give the Honeycomb a chance to live *alongside* you and make a new –

RONNIE. *Fuck* you!

CLARET. Abbie, stop!

ZANDER. *(to ABBIE)* Are you out of your mind?

ABBIE. You know how much they could share with us? You know how much they know?

CLARET. *(to ABBIE)* We already agreed, the Honeycomb agreed!

ABBIE. I didn't agree! *(to RONNIE)* They're at your mercy! You're just gonna kick them back out into the cold? "If standing up for the people who cannot stand up for themselves is not the noblest –"

RONNIE. *You're seriously quoting Dad?!* *(to CLARET)* In a million years, in a million fucking years, you think we would let you live with us?

CLARET. Only Abbie thought that. Only Abbie wanted to ask for that. The rest of us know we never could.

TANYA. Why couldn't you ask? We might say no, but you could still ask.

CLARET. After what we did to you? The shame is too much. The shame won't let us ask for any more than mercy.

RONNIE. That's funny, I didn't notice any shame until I *won*.

CLARET. *Because* you won. The *way* you won. We thought we were offering you a better life, we genuinely did, we thought we were doing a good thing. And then millions of you gave your lives in unspeakable agony throwing that offer right back at us. You couldn't have gotten all those bodies on a lie. You couldn't have won if we weren't wrong.

ABBIE. *(to RONNIE)* Can you imagine? Saying something like that? Meaning it? Ten thousand years, and they're still children.

ZANDER. I'm sorry, but could we just clarify something please? Before we get too weepy? If those eggs hatch, within minutes they'll be big enough to kill us all. Everyone in Coral Settlement, minutes.

CLARET. We won't!

ZANDER. Sure, I hear you saying that, but you could.

CLARET. Would we be physically capable? Yes, I suppose, but –

ZANDER. And this…litter of bugs that would hatch, let's say it's ten thousand, at least a hundred of those would be potential Queens. Is that right?

CLARET. I know you don't have reason to trust us –

RONNIE. Oh, you know that? That's something else millions of people died so you could know?

TANYA. Why don't you let her finish?

RONNIE. Even this? You won't even take my side on *this?*

TANYA. I'm not your enemy, Ronnie.

RONNIE. How are you not my enemy? You go against me every chance you get!

ZANDER. We're just burning time, we're burning it like we have it to lose.

TANYA. But I'm not supposed to take *your* side, right? I'm supposed to take Coral Settlement's side.

RONNIE. By letting ten thousand bug eggs hatch on our doorstep?

TANYA. We made a law against genocide. *You* made a law against genocide. Every law has a letter and a spirit.

ABBIE. Seriously?

RONNIE. *(to ABBIE.)* What, you wanna jump in here?

ABBIE. Tanya, right?

ZANDER. Ms. Miller.

TANYA. Oh, Zander, come on.

ABBIE. Tanya. What do you think you've been doing, exactly? *(to ZANDER)* What did you say, Ronnie made a famous promise? It was actually two promises, right?

Keep me safe, and when the Honeycomb's defeated, let them leave. Right?

RONNIE. You know I actually made a *point* of not telling you about that.

ABBIE. *(looking at* **FEE***)* All that time I was your prisoner, I must've asked dozens of people about Conor, until one person took pity on me.

FEE. Yeah. Taking pity on folks who don't deserve it. I used to be into that.

ABBIE. *(to* **TANYA***)* So when was that actually supposed to start happening? At what point was the defeating gonna stop and the letting-them-leave gonna start? You, Tanya, you've been living here, in Coral Settlement, under the protection of Ronnie Cooke and her bug-hunters. You go to sleep at night knowing what those bug-hunters are out there doing, what others like them doing all over the world. What have you been thinking was happening all this time? Genocide somehow isn't genocide if it's *slow?*

TANYA. All right.

ABBIE. You work for a Governor who's digging up Miami with some insane dream of turning the cable back on and setting the skyscrapers back right-side up. The Honeycomb can't live in cities. Where did you think this was all going?

TANYA. So the Honeycomb can retain the wisdom of its ancestors but we can't dig up the wisdom of ours?

> (**ZANDER** *makes a derisive sound.*)

What?

ZANDER. *(to* **RONNIE***)* Looks like she's not against you on everything.

RONNIE. No, just everyone else is.

ZANDER. We need those workers on the farms, we – What am I doing? We don't have time!

ABBIE. *(to* **RONNIE***)* Is that why you're digging up Miami? Wisdom of your ancestors?

RONNIE. Guess what? I don't have to explain myself to you!

ABBIE. Or are you looking for guns? Or gasoline?

RONNIE. You know how I got so many volunteers? How I got so many people to walk away from their families and die? Same thing, every time: I told them about the life your friends took away us.

ZANDER. Oh for god's sake –

RONNIE. The life they took away from *me, my life*! We could go anywhere, we could meet anyone, we could make anything, we could know *everything*, we could have beautiful lives! And my family took all that away, and now we have to wake up at dawn and work all day long just to have *fucking food*, and I had to give up my leg and my man and everything I ever had *cleaning up their mess*!

ZANDER. *That life isn't coming back, Ronnie!* Not for decades, maybe not for a hundred years! Look out the window: *We're farmers.* That's what we are now! Miami is under ten feet of mud! No matter what we dig out, we don't know how to use it! We're *farmers*. It's okay. We can be good farmers, we just have to say that's what we're doing. Not send people we can't spare chasing after a life we can barely remember! We have to stop talking about it, your wretched family, the ocean of shit poured on our head by the fucking Cookes. We have to stop talking about *you*. You have to let us go. We're farmers.

(**WILKIE** *enters with old, rusty paint cans.*)

WILKIE. Good to go, good to go, good to go.

ABBIE. What is that?

ZANDER. Oh look, more shit from Miami, right on cue!

ABBIE. *(trying to get close to read the label)* Lemme see it.

WILKIE. You better step the fuck back.

SHARP. You give the order, Governor.

ABBIE. Paint thinner?

RONNIE. Splash it, don't light it up yet.

WILKIE. On it, on it, on it!

SHARP. Yeah?

RONNIE. What?

SHARP. On it.

(They exit with the paint cans.)

CLARET. What's paint thinner?

ABBIE. Okay, now, paint-thinner...

RONNIE. Burns. Fast and hot. You're remembering right.

ABBIE. Wait – wait – Ronnie. What about what she said?

CLARET. Burns?

TANYA. Excuse me, I don't remember that we reached a decision.

CLARET. Burns what? *(Something out the downstage window catches her eye.)* What are they doing to her?

> *(We can hear* **SHARP** *and* **WILKIE** *splashing paint-thinner on the Queen. We hear frightened chirps and buzzes in response.)*

ZANDER. What's the alternative, Tanya?

CLARET. *(calling out the window)* Stop it! She doesn't like it! Leave her alone!

TANYA. The alternative is we *don't* commit the worst crime in the whole world!

RONNIE. All right I have had it with your *SHIT*!

> *(She grabs* **TANYA**, *flings her onto the wooden throne, and points the knife at her throat.)*

ZANDER. Governor, stop!

FEE. Ronnie!

RONNIE. Everyone get the fuck back.

TANYA. *(forcing herself to stay calm)* You can't do that, Ronnie, you can't point a knife at me.

RONNIE. See, I'd get it if it was honest, but it's really just *me*. I say something, you say the opposite, that's what you are.

TANYA. If you want to talk to me you have to put the knife down.

RONNIE. You want them to hatch? Yes or no?

TANYA. Every law has a letter and a spirit.

RONNIE. 'Cause remember this time, they *know* about the bugwater. We can't do that again. They turn on us this time, we'll have to fight them with *fucking rocks.*

TANYA. If there's a spirit to that law –

RONNIE. And you won't have Conor, and you sure as shit won't have *me,* sweetheart, I barely have two legs. And them? All *they* have to do is stay alive for twelve years and then they can birth a *million more.* So yes or no, right now: do we let them hatch?

ZANDER. This is accomplishing exactly nothing.

RONNIE. Yes or no?

TANYA. If there's a spirit to that law, it must be that there are some things so horrible, that we won't do them even in our own protection, because by doing them, we make ourselves unworthy to survive.

ABBIE. Ronnie, *please.* Isn't that true?

ZANDER. This conversation is pointless! The sun's rising! We don't have enough time to get a creature that size out of the Settlement before everyone wakes up and sees it. And nothing in the world can stop what will happen then.

TANYA. Nothing but Ronnie. If Ronnie says don't hurt her, they won't hurt her. *(to* **RONNIE***)* They won't listen to him, they won't listen to me, but they'll listen to you.

> (**RONNIE** *digs the knife in harder, but doesn't break the skin.* **TANYA** *just barely keeps it together.)*

RONNIE. And why is that?

TANYA. You know why.

RONNIE. You're fucking right I do: because I do the things you don't. I kill people, I get people to kill themselves, and when there's a choice to make, *I just make it.* That's what they respect in *me,* and what they don't see in *you.* Two kinds of people in the world: the ones who bitch about what was decided, and the ones who actually *decide!*

TANYA. Fine! Switch places with me! I'll decide!

> (**RONNIE** *lowers the knife and steps back, appraising* **TANYA**, *as* **SHARP** *and* **WILKIE** *enter.*)

RONNIE. *(indicating* **ABBIE** *and* **CLARET***)* Secure them.

WILKIE. My pleasure.

> (*Over the following,* **WILKIE** *grabs* **ABBIE** *and struggles to tie his hands, but* **ABBIE** *breaks away.*)

ABBIE. Ronnie! Jesus Christ! It's mass murder!

RONNIE. Yeah, tell me about mass murder.

SHARP. *(to* **CLARET***)* Come on, now.

CLARET. Ronnie Cooke, please!

SHARP. *(pulling her away from the window)* Come on, now.

ABBIE. You've gotta find some forgiveness, Ronnie, I know it's hard, but you've gotta find some forgiveness!

RONNIE. *(to* **WILKIE**, *meaning the wall of names)* Put him on the Wall!

> (**WILKIE** *slams* **ABBIE** *against the wall of names.*)

Touch his name. Put your hand on it.

ABBIE. Peck?

RONNIE. Conor!

ABBIE. Ronnie, look, if I said some things, if I let my temper –

RONNIE. Put your hand on his name!

> (**ABBIE** *touches Conor's name.*)

Now forgive *me.* I sent him to his death on a lie. Say you forgive *me.* Let's see if you can say it. To save an entire race? I bet you could even sound like you mean it.

> (**RONNIE** *touches* **PECK**'s *name.*)

He used to pick me up in the air and just hold me there. His arms were like the whole world. Only times in my life that I didn't have to be who I am. *(to* **WILKIE***)* Gag him.

WILKIE. On it!

ABBIE. Wait wait Ronnie come on, I forgive you, all right, I –

*(***WILKIE*** gags ***ABBIE*** and puts him on his knees.)*

RONNIE. *(to* **SHARP***)* Her too.

SHARP. Yeah.

CLARET. *Ronnie Cooke!*

*(***RONNIE*** looks at her.)*

I'm an anthropologist. I study humans. I've never known anything so fascinating. And I've noticed, in my studies, that humans do this. *(She gets down on her knees.)* This is what you do, yes? To make yourself lower than the one to whom you are supplicating? Please, Ronnie Cooke. Please don't kill my people. I beg you, I *beg* you, we were wrong, but we can be right! We can be humble, we can learn, we can be better than we were, please don't kill our babies! I'm sorry we hurt you but please forgive us, please don't kill our babies, please let us try again!

FEE. *(going to* **CLARET***)* She's right, Ronnie. You can't kill their babies. Nothing would be worse than if you killed their babies.

RONNIE. Fee, why don't you –

FEE. *(to* **CLARET***)* 'Cause in the Time Before, I wouldn't have lost *my* babies. With the hospitals they used to have? I'd still have all five of my babies. Not dead in that longboat next to her four babies that lived. *(indicating* **RONNIE***)* Same food, same water, same blankets, but all five of my babies took sick while all four of her babies got strong. And all four of her babies lived while all *five* of my babies died!

CLARET. I'm so sorry.

FEE. *(to* **CLARET***)* You're so sorry? I could be raising my babies right now, not hers! They wouldn't ask for her every single day 'cause they'd be *mine*. I wouldn't be following after her, rubbing her fucked-up leg, raising her fucked-up baby Shirley that she never sees. I'd have *my babies* instead of watching them take sick and die on that boat 'cause there was a world that could've saved them and *you* took it away!

CLARET. Yes, I hear you.

FEE. You *hear* me?!

CLARET. *(meaning the Queen)* I hear you, and I say to you in turn, with the greatest respect for your sorrow, that she loves her babies as much as you love yours.

FEE. Fuck you.

CLARET. She loves her babies as much as you loved yours.

FEE. *Fuck you!*

CLARET. They don't look like your babies, but she loves them just the same.

(*pause*)

RONNIE. Fee?

FEE. I don't know, Ronnie.

ZANDER. Governor, everyone who comes before our court tells their little story and every one of them cries. Tears are easy. As easy as it will be for them to kill us all the minute they hatch.

(**RONNIE** *turns to* **SHARP** *and* **WILKIE**.)

WILKIE. We're ready on your say.

RONNIE. Sharp?

SHARP. I'll follow any order you give.

WILKIE. Let's do this.

RONNIE. *(to* **SHARP***)* Sharp?

(*beat*)

SHARP. One thing we do sometimes is plant the fleshy flowers in a break in the trees. They can't help themselves, they wanna drink even if they know it's a trap. Formation drops down into the trees, and then two of them, every time, turn their bellies into our spears while the others drink and get away. Turn at the same time, at the same speed, and I've never figured out how they decide which two. I hate them. I hunt them. I kill them. They're perfect.

> *(silence)*

RONNIE. Who's got a torch outside?

WILKIE. Bunch of the guys, why?

RONNIE. *(to SHARP, referring to TANYA)* Watch her.

> *(She exits out the front door.)*

WILKIE. *(as RONNIE exits)* Wait, what are you – Governor, we'll do it, what're you –

CLARET. *RONNIE COOKE!*

> *(WILKIE ties the gag around CLARET's mouth.)*

TANYA. Zander?

> *(ZANDER sits down and looks away from her.)*

It's just me? It's just *me*?

> *(She runs for the front door. SHARP intercepts her easily.)*

Let me go!

SHARP. Be easy.

TANYA. Let me *go*! Governor!

SHARP. Easy.

TANYA. *(calling out the door)* Ronnie!

> *(The sound of flames igniting. The stage lights up yellow and orange. Horrible, inhuman buzzing shrieks from outside. CLARET lies on the floor wailing into her gag. ZANDER turns upstage in his chair. FEE stands at the window, looking out. New noises as the flames burn through the ropes holding the Queen. We hear it thrashing around outside. The eggs, burning.)*

WILKIE. Should we get out there?

SHARP. Wait.

> *(The buzzing and thrashing sounds get weaker and weaker, eventually ceasing.)*

WILKIE. Do you see her?

SHARP. Wait.

WILKIE. I don't see her.

> *(**WILKIE** starts for the door.)*

SHARP. Wait.

> *(**RONNIE** enters.)*

RONNIE. Help me.

> *(**WILKIE** goes to her and supports her.)*

RONNIE. My chair.

> *(**WILKIE** helps her to her chair. **ABBIE**, still gagged, makes a furious, broken noise and lunges at **RONNIE**. **SHARP** restrains him.)*

RONNIE. Let him go.

SHARP. Don't think so.

RONNIE. Let him go.

SHARP. Not gonna happen.

> *(The energy goes out of **ABBIE**. **SHARP** removes his gag. Over the following, **ABBIE** goes to **CLARET** and holds her.)*

RONNIE. Folks are gonna be coming out. Get some teams together, we need crowd control.

SHARP. *(to **WILKIE**)* Come on.

WILKIE. *(meaning **ABBIE** and **CLARET**)* What about them?

RONNIE. They're finished.

> *(**SHARP** and **WILKIE** exit. **FEE** pulls a chair over to **RONNIE**.)*

FEE. Give it to me.

> *(She rests **RONNIE**'s leg on her thighs and massages it.)*

RONNIE. You okay?

FEE. I'm sorry for what I said.

RONNIE. Why?

FEE. Is this helping?

RONNIE. Zander.

ZANDER. Mm. Yeah, yes, sorry.

RONNIE. Fee can be the witness.

ZANDER. Witness to what?

RONNIE. Me handing over Governor to you. *(pause)*

ZANDER. Wait.

FEE. What?

RONNIE. You want it or not?

FEE. Ronnie, wait a day, wait a couple of days.

RONNIE. I'll swear you in right now. Fee can be witness. If Fee's witness people will know it's honest.

ZANDER. Why would you do that?

RONNIE. 'Cause I want something.

ZANDER. Conditions.

RONNIE. Three.

ZANDER. Go ahead.

RONNIE. Skin goes free. She can stay if she wants or not. But nobody ever knows.

ZANDER. I'd have to keep her under watch for a while.

RONNIE. Whatever.

ZANDER. What else?

RONNIE. If you're Governor we need a Manager.

ZANDER. Sure, I can put forward some candidates...

(He realizes **RONNIE** *is looking at* **TANYA.***)*

No. Come on, Ronnie, Governor, no. What are you doing? You can't stand her!

TANYA. You can't do that, Governor.

RONNIE. *(to* **ZANDER***)* Yes or no?

TANYA. Governor, I'm telling you now, if you give me that position, I'm gonna charge you with genocide.

RONNIE. I'm talking to him.

TANYA. No, first I'm gonna ask the Council for amnesty for every one of the Transitioned in our prison. I'm gonna get the votes, I'm gonna give them language, and I'm gonna make them citizens of this settlement! Do you hear me?

RONNIE. You want the gig or not?

TANYA. And then I'm gonna charge you with genocide, I'm gonna get the guilty finding, and I'm gonna see you executed with honor!

RONNIE. *(to* **TANYA***)* You want the gig or not?

TANYA. Yes. I want it.

     *(***RONNIE** *looks at* **ZANDER.***)*

ZANDER. She'll make my life a nightmare.

RONNIE. *(to* **ZANDER***)* Yes or no?

ZANDER. All right! God, I can only imagine what's next.

RONNIE. I execute Abbie. Myself. In this room. Nobody else.

ZANDER. No. Not acceptable.

RONNIE. Or you don't get to be Governor.

ZANDER. I have to do it myself. It can be just the three of us, that's fine, but if I'm going to be Governor I have to be able to tell these people that I killed Abbie Cooke. I have to be able to say I killed *someone.*

RONNIE. All right.

FEE. Ronnie. Get some sleep and decide this tomorrow.

RONNIE. When does Shirley wake up?

FEE. Soon, I guess. With the sun.

RONNIE. Then we should do this so you can get home.

FEE. Are you sure?

RONNIE. On my side.

     *(***FEE** *helps* **RONNIE** *stand. To* **ZANDER***:)*

Get the thing.

     *(***ZANDER** *gets the Law book.)*

ZANDER. You know, we don't really have a process for this. People just sort of carried you in here.

RONNIE. Come on.

ZANDER. I'm definitely going to institute some regular practices around here.

RONNIE. Put your hand on it. Zander Smith, do you swear to obey and enforce the laws of Coral Settlement?

ZANDER. I do.

RONNIE. Do you swear to serve the People of Coral Settlement with every resource at your command?

ZANDER. I do.

FEE. Ronnie…

RONNIE. Then I grant you the title of Governor of Coral Settlement. *(to* **ZANDER**, *indicating* **TANYA***)* Think you can repeat that?

ZANDER. Ms. Miller?

> *(***ZANDER*** goes to swear in* **TANYA** **RONNIE** *and* **FEE** *move a little bit away.)*

Tanya Miller, do you swear to obey and enforce the laws of Coral Settlement?

TANYA. I do.

RONNIE. *(to* **FEE***)* Go home. Tell Shirley I asked about her.

ZANDER. Do you swear to serve the People of Coral Settlement with every resource at your command?

TANYA. I do.

FEE. Tomorrow?

RONNIE. Yeah.

ZANDER. Then I grant you the title of Manager of Coral Settlement.

> *(***SHARP** *and* **WILKIE** *return.* **TANYA** *goes to undo* **CLARET***'s gag.* **FEE** *leaves over the following.)*

SHARP. We've got some men in place but we'll need to get back out there.

WILKIE. People are starting to come up. Like, lots of people.

RONNIE. Yeah.

(As **FEE** *is leaving, there are sounds of cheers outside.)*

ZANDER. What's happening out there?

WILKIE. Burned up Queen, man, people are celebrating!

TANYA. *(to* **CLARET***)* Come with me. *(to* **RONNIE***)* Ronnie?

ABBIE. Go with her.

RONNIE. *(to* **SHARP** *and* **WILKIE***)* It's okay.

*(***WILKIE*** goes to* **CLARET** *and unties her over the following.)*

CLARET. No.

ABBIE. Go with her, it's all right.

CLARET. I don't want to, I want to die.

ABBIE. No you don't.

CLARET. I do.

ABBIE. You don't. The baby.

CLARET. I can't do it.

ABBIE. You have to. You're a Queen now.

CLARET. I can't.

TANYA. Claret.

*(***CLARET*** turns to her.)*

What small thing will you do to help build the Honeycomb?

CLARET. What?

TANYA. There's hundreds of Transitioned in our prison right now. They need to learn to walk, they need language, and they need to learn to write. Do you think you can help me?

CLARET. Write?

TANYA. Of course. How can we preserve the story of the Honeycomb for our children if they don't write it down?

CLARET. It won't work.

TANYA. Of course it will.

CLARET. Honeycomb memories are perfect recordings, it's like they're happening *as* you remember them. That's gone now. We'll remember things wrong, we'll disagree over details, we'll change things to make ourselves sound better. They'll be human memories.

TANYA. Then they'll be human memories. That's what's left.

CLARET. *(to* ABBIE*)* I'll name the baby your name. You do that, yes, that's a custom?

ABBIE. You can't.

CLARET. I'll give it your name!

ABBIE. You can't call a baby Abbie. Not anymore.

> *(He kisses her.)*

Get her out of here.

CLARET. But…

TANYA. *(to* CLARET*)* Come with me now.

CLARET. Abbie.

ABBIE. Goodbye, Claret.

TANYA. *(to* RONNIE*)* You'll be hearing from me.

> *(She and* CLARET *exit.)*

WILKIE. Man, fuck her. Fuck both of 'em.

RONNIE. Lookin' a little crazy out there.

SHARP. Come on, Wilkie.

WILKIE. I'll catch up.

RONNIE. Sharp.

> *(They look at each other.)*

SHARP. Yeah.

> *(He exits.)*

WILKIE. Hey, hey. You know I have your back, right?

RONNIE. Yeah, Wilkie.

WILKIE. People say shit, I say forget them. You're Ronnie Cooke. You don't answer to anybody. C'mere. *(He kisses her.)* I'm gonna be there for you. You know that, right?

No matter what. I know you had that other guy before, I'm not trying to be that guy, but I can be a different guy. I can be the guy from now on. Whatever you need, I'm on it.

RONNIE. Thank you, Wilkie.

WILKIE. You know that, right?

RONNIE. Help Sharp out.

WILKIE. I'll see you later?

RONNIE. Yeah.

> *(WILKIE leaves. RONNIE and ZANDER are alone with ABBIE.)*

ZANDER. Ronnie, you know there won't be any trial, right? I mean obviously there wouldn't be any popular support – they'd probably burn her house down just for making the charge.

RONNIE. *(drawing her knife)* Ready?

ZANDER. Just like that?

RONNIE. *(to ABBIE)* Anything to say first?

ABBIE. I hope you never feel love again for as long as you live.

> *(beat)*

RONNIE. *(to ZANDER)* You're up.

ZANDER. Right. All right. So I just… I mean it's easy, right?

RONNIE. If you knock him out he won't be looking at you.

ZANDER. I can do that?

RONNIE. You know how to knock somebody out, Governor?

ZANDER. You know I don't.

RONNIE. *(casually ambling behind ZANDER)* You want the brain to hit the side of the skull, so you need their head to snap to one side fast. I like the punch to the jaw myself.

ZANDER. *(miming a punch)* You mean like this?

RONNIE. No.

(She punches ZANDER *in the head, knocking him unconscious. She hobbles to where the bug-hunter cloaks are hanging.)*

ABBIE. What…what's happening?

RONNIE. *(throwing a cloak at him)* Put it on.

ABBIE. I don't understand.

RONNIE. You don't understand what?

*(*ABBIE *puts the cloak on.* RONNIE *indicates the far end of the room.)*

RONNIE. Drag him over there real quick and then you can take off.

ABBIE. Take off?

RONNIE. Just right there and then you can go. Come on! I can't do it!

*(*ABBIE *numbly drags* ZANDER *along the floor.)*

ABBIE. Here?

RONNIE. All the way, against the wall.

*(*ABBIE *drags* ZANDER *to the far end of the room as* RONNIE *takes the thermos off the memory wall.)*

RONNIE. Great, you're done. Go. *(pause)* What? Do we have anything to say to each other?

ABBIE. No.

RONNIE. The only way you're walking out of this house is if everyone in the Settlement is looking in another direction. You've got 'til the fire stops.

ABBIE. *(looking at* ZANDER*)* Wait, why did I just –

RONNIE. Get out!

*(*ABBIE *goes to the door and then stops.)*

ABBIE. Ronnie?

RONNIE. The fuck are you still doing here?

ABBIE. I dragged him more than ten paces.

RONNIE. Out! Now!

ABBIE. Did I just drag him out of the blast radius?

(They look at each other.)

ABBIE. What's in the thermos?

RONNIE. Contingency. In case the bugs ever tried to take the Governor alive.

ABBIE. Oh. *(pause)*

RONNIE. It's what right, isn't it?

ABBIE. Yes.

RONNIE. Then what are we talking about?

ABBIE. Nothing. Goodbye.

RONNIE. Yeah.

> **(ABBIE** *exits.* **RONNIE** *goes to the wall and touches Peck's name.)*

RONNIE. Are you with me?

> *(She unscrews the thermos and raises it to her lips just as* **ABBIE** *comes back in and seizes her wrist.)*

RONNIE. Hey – hey! The fuck – !

> **(ABBIE** *wrests the thermos from her and throws it on the ground. He embraces her.* **RONNIE** *struggles, fiercely.)*

RONNIE. No – no – no – NO – NO!

> *(Then the fight goes out of her. She holds on to* **ABBIE.** *She pushes her face into his chest. They hold each other like lost children. Then* **ABBIE** *detaches, goes to the cloaks.)*

RONNIE. What…?

ABBIE. *(throwing* **RONNIE** *a cloak)* Put it on. We have to go.

RONNIE. *(putting the cloak on)* My leg.

ABBIE. Shit. *(He's looking around the room.)* Wait.

> *(He runs and grabs one of the reapers. He puts the blade end on the floor and stamps on it until the blade breaks off. He holds it out to* **RONNIE.**)

Walking stick. No one'll ever think it's you.

(She takes the walking stick. He helps her walk to the front door. Then he stops.)

RONNIE. What?

ABBIE. We can't go out there.

RONNIE. No, we can, they're watching the fire.

ABBIE. No, I mean, we can't go out on the porch. I saw the Bald Woman.

RONNIE. Oh, fuck you.

ABBIE. I swear! I saw her on the porch!

RONNIE. Fuck you.

ABBIE. She's crawling across the porch, right now, I swear!

RONNIE. I don't believe you.

ABBIE. You're not scared?

RONNIE. She's not out there.

ABBIE. Then tell me to open this door. If she's not out there, tell me to open this door.

RONNIE. Open it.

(lights down)

End of Play

Lightning Source UK Ltd.
Milton Keynes UK
UKHW020936120920
369736UK00005B/395